SEE WHAT READERS SAY

"Jim Carroll, using historical fiction set in today's current Middle Eastern context, tells a riveting story about the drive to succeed, prophetic dreams, friendship, arrests and even death threats as part of the life-revealing message of Christian hope. Reading *HOT SPOT* was for me, an experience that was both instructive and intensely interesting. I recommend this book for the person investigating Christianity and for those seeking to understand some of the ways the message of Christianity is effectively spreading around the world."

– Rev. Michael Hearon
1st Presbyterian Church, Augusta, Georgia, Lead Pastor

"Rich detail and an engaging plot are a winning combination for *HOT SPOT*, Jim Carroll's latest novel, highlighting the fascinating and often dangerous life of a Christian living in a Muslim country."

– Laurie Myers
Author, *The Shepherd's Song, The Lord is Their Shepherd,* and
Be Strong in the Lord

"From his first-hand knowledge of the Middle East, Dr. Carroll delivers a fast-paced thriller full of surprises. A young man must make messy choices that injure his conscience and must make bold decisions that affect millions. A

of God in history, cultures, and individuals. I can't wait for the sequel."

– Jerry A. Miller, Jr, MD
Author, *The Burden of Being Champ: The Dropout, The Legend, and The Pediatrician*

"Yet another novel from the pen of Dr. James Carroll, recounting the intricacies of life in the Middle East. Through this tale, you'll learn about the dynamic relationships inside Kuwaiti families and the challenges of the young generation trying to balance Eastern tradition with Western values, all told from the lives of a tiny Christian minority in a nation ruled by the strictest Islamic laws. Carroll brings us a greater understanding of the Sunni/Shia tension that exists between Muslims today. Set against the backdrop of current historical and geo-political events, the reader is instantly drawn into a plot which highlights how the Lord brings his elect from among the Arabs. Once you pick up this book, you will not be able to put it down."

– John Kaddis, MD
US physician, Raised in the Middle East

"*HOT SPOT* depicts the life of a Middle Eastern Christian man living in a Muslim world. I was surprised at how riveted I was reading about his battles within society as well as within himself when he believed he was not following the God of his Christian faith. Though Dr. Carroll makes clear this book is fictional, I believe this portrayal is quite true to life for the many Muslims who are coming to see Jesus as their true Savior, oftentimes through dreams, and thus facing the persecution and punishments for their beliefs. This was a great read, and an eye opener for those who might take their gift of faith for granted in our comfortable and nominally Christian Western world!"

– Doreen Hung Mar, MD
Mission to the World Medical Associate Missionary

HOT SPOT

A TURBULENT MODERN STORY
IN AN ANCIENT LAND

JIM CARROLL

HigherLife Development Services, Inc.

P.O. Box 623307

Oviedo, Florida 32762

(407) 563-4806

www.ahigherlife.com

Printed in Canada

10 9 8 7 6 5 4 3 2 1

Carroll, Jim

Hot Spot: A Turbulent Modern Story in an Ancient Land

ISBN # 978-1-7326377-9-5 (paperback)

ISBN # 978-1-7328859-0-5 (ebook)

ACKNOWLEDGMENTS

I want to thank my editor, Ellen King, for her thorough and thoughtful work on my novel. Without her help, the story would have lagged and lacked clarity. I appreciated her close communication with me during the process.

This is a work of fiction. Although most of the history and some of the people are factual, names, characters, businesses, places, events, locales, and incidents are either the products of the author's imagination or used in a fictitious manner.

LIST OF CHARACTERS

Yusef – primary character

Rabea – mother of Yusef

Yacoub – father of Yusef

Hibah – Yusef's older sister

Binyamin – Yusef's younger brother

Divina – the family's faithful maid

Esau –Yusef's half brother

Dhuwaihi – old man who became a Christian, friend of the family

John Freidecker – American Christian and longtime resident of Kuwait

Afsin – Yusef's first convert in Iran, young son of his host family

Abbas and Shaheen – Iranian converts to Christianity

Mahmoud Rashidi – director of the Iranian Researches and Foreign Relations office – Yusef's first ministry boss

Karim Khadim – head of the Ministry of Economic Affairs and Finance – Yusef's big boss

Tahara – Al Jazeera female reporter admired by Yusef

SOME UNFAMILIAR WORDS

Abaya – black robe worn by conservative Arab women

Chador - a black robe covering the head and upper body, often worn in Iran

Dishdasha – Kuwaiti word for the typical men's robe

Dīwāniya sessions – unique Kuwaiti custom consisting of men's discussion groups

Fatwa – an Islamic ruling

Kafan – Islamic shroud for the dead

Kalb – Arabic for "dog"

Kafir – the Islamic term for an unbeliever (or disbeliever)

Keffiyeh – standard head covering for Kuwaiti men

Muezzin – the one who calls the faithful for Islamic prayer

Niqab – garment that covers the face

Oud – a lute-like instrument with 11 or 13 strings

Salat – prayer

Ṣalāt al-Janāzah – Islamic prayers for the dead

Sharia – Islamic law

Shawarma or shaurma – a street food consisting of flatbread, lettuce, tomatoes, and meat shaved from grilled meat

Thobe or thawb – other words used for the typical robe

Wudu – Islamic procedure for washing parts of the body in preparation for prayer

MAP OF THE MIDDLE EAST[1]

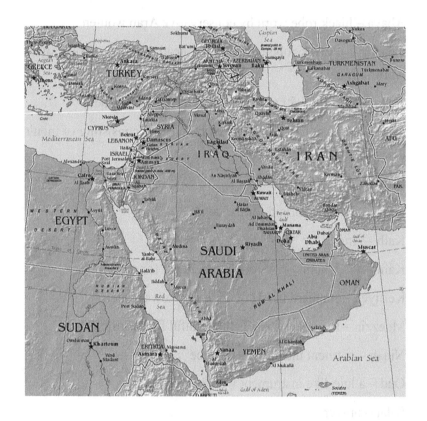

1 "Physical Map of the Middle East," Www.cia.gov/library/publications/resources/the-world-factbook/attachments/docs/original/middle_east.pdf?1528326232, accessed November 20, 2018, www.cia.gov/library/publications/resources/the-world-factbook/attachments/docs/original/middle_east.pdf?1528326232.

PREFACE

The Middle East is mired in its own history, both ancient and modern. I can tell no story of this land without placing the events in the context of the history from which they sprang. You could skip those parts of this story, but I advise against it.

CHAPTER 1

DEAD TOO SOON

I never thought of myself as a Muslim. My mother taught us that the Lord was full of grace and forgiveness because Jesus had taken the punishment we deserved, but we were known as Christians only at home and among a few other believers, a very small group. We appeared in the Kuwait public arena as Muslims who did not practice their faith. We were closeted Christians. When the Prophet Mohammed was discussed, we refrained from critical comments. During Ramadan, we didn't eat or drink in public. Once a schoolmate caught me in a corner choking down a sandwich at recess during Ramadan. "What are you doing? You can't eat during the day." But I could and did. Carefully.

We were wealthy, and traveled in expensive cars: a black Lexus, a big white Mercedes, and a monster Suburban when we needed more seating. If more cars were needed, we bought them. The bronze gate that opened into our watered garden with its aerated fountain greeted our guests. Our Pakistani gatekeeper welcomed them. There was no doubt about it. We were rich, just as rich as our Muslim neighbors.

###

Our home glowed with the presence of my mother, who illuminated each room with her dignity. Her entry into any room of the house was punctuated by her greeting, "May the Lord's blessings be with you!" She infused this into us from our earliest days. Meals were a time of quiet rejoicing: "See what the Lord has brought us today. Hibah and Yusef, stop elbowing each other. Respect the gifts of Jesus." My father needed to say little. Early on in my life, my mother recognized my weaknesses, especially my pride. "Yusef, remember you're the youngest. Don't keep pestering your sister." My bedtime was directed by my mother, and she settled me in each evening with her prayers. "Lord, bless this little one and keep him safe from Your enemies, as well as himself."

My other childhood recollections with my mother still under our roof are cloudy and somewhat warped by my stubborn refusal to accept her beliefs as my own. As she saw clearly, my opinion of myself was elevated above the level of reality.

I recall hearing my parents talking about me as I listened from the hall behind the green curtain as a small child. I didn't understand it then, but it still remains frozen in my mind. "Yacoub," my mother was saying, "I know Yusef's only five, but he's focused too much on himself. Everybody praises him and he believes every word of it! He is taking advantage of you and you don't see it because you're so proud of him. He parrots Scripture, and while I don't expect him to understand them fully, he is not storing their meaning in his heart. I know the Word of God will not fail him, but he isn't submitting to God" As a child I didn't understand what she was saying, but the words hurt.

4

My mother was the kindest, most patient person I've ever known. When father foolishly fawned over me, she remained silent. She was tolerant and forgiving toward both of us, but she didn't agree with my father's opinions. My mother saw the truth about me. When my father cited my remarkable memorization of Scripture, she quoted the first half of Romans 10:10, "For with the heart one believes," not so much to voice her worry, but to speak forth her hope for me. My mother prayed for my future, even though I did not understand the need for it then.

I always had my father completely in hand. My assertive carriage; dark, curly hair; good looks attested to by all around; and endearing personality all served me well. I was often told as much directly. Auntie Zahara said, "He's more beautiful than any of our daughters." Even as a small child, my abilities at soccer also made me the center of attention: *Look, he just made another goal!*

To compound the problem, I had another special ability. I could foresee future events and the actions of others. It was not constant and I could not call on it at will, but it was there. Perhaps this skill had to do with my morning dreams, much like the ones my father experienced.

I recall the morning of my fifth birthday. At breakfast I announced, "Papa, I dreamed last night that I will be king of the all the Gulf." He laughed and told me to stop bragging, but it was not a serious rebuke. Everyone knew I was his favorite. Oftentimes, my father treated my sister unfairly. She did not get the same attention I did or the same recognition. When I made this announcement, she sat silently looking at me, her arms folded across her chest. She knew that Father would get angry if she countered me. Instead she conferred with my mother later on.

By dinner time, the whole matter of my self-centeredness had reached an embarrassing climax. Our longtime Philippine maid, Divina, delivered the lentil soup, light green and thick, to begin the meal. All were silent, having recognized the issue at hand, as yet unspoken. Then Divina brought out the quail, imported from Egypt, and my mouth watered at the sight of their brown, crusty skin. But my kingly claims transcended even this wonderful meal before us. My mother spoke up, plowing in to it in the only time we could discuss this as a family. In an instant, all her hopes and fears erupted. "Yacoub, Yusef's doing it again. He told this dream of his being king of the Gulf. These ideas aren't healthy for him, and he does not admit to making it all up either. He may really believe these dreams he has are real!" My father said nothing. I didn't want the quail any longer.

###

My mother taught me the Scriptures early in my life focusing on the book of Psalms, and I stored it away like it was a recording on tape. I answered biblical questions with an understanding greater than my years, and people told me how intelligent and advanced I was. I was proud of my achievements, but Mother shook her head at my pretending to store the material in my heart. How did she see through me so clearly? "Yusef, today you will memorize Psalm 47." Always, it was a psalm. She prayed aloud, "Please, Lord, use Your Word to immunize this child against his own strong will. Save him from himself. I know You've given him gifts for Your purpose. I pray his gifts won't cancel out Your Word. You know what's best, Lord; protect and keep him. I'm afraid of what the future holds for my little boy, but we will trust in You." There was no such fear in me. My father deferred to my mother in matters of faith. When she spoke thus, he said nothing.

Looking back, I see how diminished I was by her death when I was thirteen. Her name, Rabea, meant "springtime" in Arabic, and she was that and more for my father and our whole family.

Our joy came first. She was pregnant! My parents had wanted another child for some time, and as she was nearing fifty, they had long put the hope aside. They thought it was too late for a child, but God intervened.

My mother immediately had to spend more time in bed, and I quickly regretted the unborn baby's intrusion into the center of my realm. She developed high blood pressure, and the doctor found it difficult to treat. Pill bottles multiplied by her bedside table: pink tablets, blue capsules. She would normally avoid this kind of thing at all costs. The doctor eventually put her on full bed rest. Then, an ultrasound revealed that the placenta was not properly attached. The doctor showed us the grainy picture of a baby boy on the ultrasound. "What you see here is that the placenta is nearly on top of the cervix. When delivery comes, there could be a lot of bleeding." I peered over my father's shoulder, seeing only meaningless black and gray images, but their low voices and solemn faces made me afraid. At the beginning of the eighth month I heard my mother groaning in the bathroom. What did this mean? Hibah's face lost its color, and she wouldn't answer my questions.

My mother said, "These are only the normal cramps every woman gets before labor." But I had not seen her ever complain of pain, and I knew something was wrong. She minimized the situation, "I'm sure it's nothing, just what's expected with pregnancy in an old woman." She tried to cover the pain, but her straight-lipped expression and worried eyes betrayed her concern. Could my mother be afraid? Why was she so troubled?

She talked by phone with her mother in Saudi. They had not spoken for years, and her mother was nearly eighty. I listened as they talked. "It's good, Mama, to speak with you finally." Then she began to cry. "I'm sorry for stealing your gold." When my mother had married my father, she had taken gold from her mother. She had wanted to punish her for allowing the marriage to my father when she was not yet out of childhood.

From what I could hear of the conversation, her mother was gentle and forgiving about the theft. "Mother, I know now you didn't want the marriage, and I don't blame you for it anymore. I've grown into it. Yacoub is a good man. I'm so sorry for the time we lost together." The phone call between the two women was long. When my mother said goodbye, she didn't promise another conversation.

Then, in late November at three in the morning, loud voices

8

flared from my parents' room. I peered through the half-open door. My mother was in bed shaking from head to foot, her face red with the strain, forehead veins distended. Divina said, "She's having a convulsion." Mama's head was thrown back and her arms and legs extended and shook rhythmically. Her head was forcefully turned to the left. I had never seen anything like this before, not even in movies, and I was afraid. After an endless two-to-three minutes the shaking stopped, but she remained unconscious.

"We've got to get her to the hospital." Divina helped my father carry my mother and place her in the second seat of our Suburban, to go to Al-Sabah Maternity Hospital down by the sea. Hibah and I begged to go, and Divina relented, pushing us in the third seat of the big white vehicle. The two of us were out of our element, trembling with fear.

My mother had another convulsion on the way to the hospital. We heard her head pounding against the seat back. Hibah cried while I turned and hid my face in the gray leather. The scene consumed my thirteen-year-old bravery. I had no courage left by the time we reached the hospital.

My father had never met the Sikh doctor on call that night, but there was no alternative but to trust him. "Get her back to delivery – now." The nurses listened with wide eyes to his commands. *Had they not seen him so excited before?* The adults pushed us aside while leads were attached to Mama's chest and lower abdomen over the baby. The doctor explained that the convulsions were caused by her high blood pressure. He used the word "eclampsia": an unfamiliar word that silenced us with its fearful, medical sound. The next thing we heard was, "We must deliver this baby right away." Blood began to stain the lower part of Mama's sheet. At the doctor's order, two white-clad nurses with starched caps pushed her gurney into the delivery room.

Thirty minutes later, the doctor came out to the small waiting room, and said the baby boy was fine. My worry stopped for a moment. Then, to my father he said, "I can't get the bleeding stopped unless we operate." Since it was my father's place, as the Arab man, to make the choice of life or death for my mother, the doctor asked his permission to remove the uterus.

But events moved too fast. My father ran into the operating theater with the doctor. *Was it too late?* Thirty minutes later my father summoned us all into the room with its bright lights, two IV bags with clear fluids, and one with a thick red liquid, which I guessed was blood, and shiny steel tools still open next to my mother. Her skin was like a clean white bed sheet. She spoke to my father only, but we all heard, "Yacoub, you and the children must take this land." Then she recited Psalm 63:1: "O God, you are my God, earnestly I seek you; my soul thirsts for you; my flesh faints for you, as in a dry and parched land where there is no water." She slipped away right in front of us. Just like that – our mother was gone. *Why, Lord, did you take her so soon?* A thirteen-year-old should not see this.

I couldn't bear it. I was seeing adult events, and I wasn't ready.

An hour later, Divina took us again into the hospital room to see our mother one last time. We went in together, Papa following, head bowed. The tubes and IVs had been removed, her hands were folded over her abdomen and outside the cover, and she looked as if she slept quietly. Her peaceful expression gave me a moment of hope, but hope for what? I wasn't sure. I just wanted everything to be the same again.

My father stated joylessly that the baby's name would Binya-min. I could only ask, "Why Binya-min?" All Arab names are selected for their meaning. My father intended one of the ancient meanings of the name: "the son of my old age."

My father requested the ward attendants to care for her body, and two female attendants hurried into my mother's room, both anxious to serve our rich family. Divina remembered there was a Christian cemetery in Fahaheel near Ahmadi, and asked the nurses to get the body ready for transfer to the funeral home there. "We'll take her to the Fahaheel Christian Cemetery."

The nurses proceeded at first as we requested, but a few minutes later, a tall man strode in with his hands on his hips. His long beard and shorter than usual dishdasha were indicative of the most conservative Islamic views, supposedly an emulation of the dress of the Prophet. "We have firm rules about burial for Muslims. As hospital administrator, I must see those rules observed. As a Muslim, she must be buried according to Sharia." He nodded with an order to Divina. "Please proceed now with the washing of the body."

Divina paled. My father turned to face the man and block the way. They saw my own stunned expression. Too old to cry in front of strangers, I turned to my father, "Papa, what's happening? Mama's not a Muslim. She teaches me the psalms. She loves Jesus." The secret spilled out.

Two long-bearded hospital guards appeared at the door. The administrator looked at me as he glanced back at the clock. "Mr. Al-Tamimi, please control your family. If not, I'll summon the proper authorities from the Ministry of Islamic Affairs. Your wife was an Arab woman born here in Kuwait. She is therefore Muslim. We must follow Sharia. She cannot be buried like a *kefer* (unbeliever)." The guards pushed Hibah and me out the door and into the lobby.

I resisted, "You must let us take my mother. She's already with Jesus. You can't have her."

Divina had no choice. She must have done as they instructed, because when we were allowed back into the room, momma was wrapped in the *kafan* for burial provided by the hospital. Victorious, the administrator presented a kinder demeanor. "I'm sorry for your loss. We know you're confused. We'll take care of the body for you. I trust you'll gather your family for the *Salat al-Janazah* (the prayers for forgiveness of the dead)."

I spoke again out of turn, "Mama's already forgiven. Your prayers are for those not forgiven." The administrator glared at me, as if I was a disobedient child. My father was too stricken to respond. I stiffened. *Would this man hit me?*

The guards ushered us out to our car, and no choice was offered to us. Divina carried little Binyamin wrapped in a blue hospital blanket. The rest of us couldn't look at him. We were told our mother's body would be taken to the Muslim cemetery at Sulaibikhat and that she would be buried within twenty-four hours according to Islamic tradition. Hibah was silent and stone-faced. I wanted only my youthful sense of justice satisfied. "They've stolen Mother's body. Papa, what are you going to do?" The silent answer was nothing. We had no rights in the matter.

I balled up my fists in recognition of our weakness. My father made no attempt to explain or argue with me. My adolescent views counted for nothing, and they were worth nothing. After all, what could a teen do about the imminent mistreatment of his mother's body? Except for my innocent, lonely jeremiad, everyone was silent on the drive back to Ahmadi, but I resolved that I would fight this, perhaps not now, but later.

I had never observed my mother to fear death, but she did fear leaving us to our own devices, and probably for good reason. Many times I'd heard that from her in some form or another. I encouraged myself with the fact that she was taking Muslim ground for her grave as a down payment on the rest of the land.

After we arrived home in Ahmadi, Divina assumed an authoritative role. As we entered the door, she gave orders for our duties. And as if God wanted to make it worse, a dust storm arose, stinging sand following us into the house. "Yusef, go to your room and make your bed. Hibah, sit with your father on his lap for now." My father sat with a face like ice, no tears, and no arms around Hibah, who looked down and stared at the floor.

Father was unable to function in any role for several weeks, and Binyamin received little attention from us in the beginning. We relegated him to Divina's arms, as if to comfort him would be betrayal of our dead mother. We blamed him for taking her from us. Even my father seemed not to see the little one. Binyamin's cries were heeded only by Divina. I still couldn't look at him; he was only the instrument of my mother's demise to me.

I ignored my playmates and even Hibah and Father for months after Mama's death. I blamed everyone, including myself. My dreams increased in frequency and variety. I had dreams about my own death, visions of future successes, and of being pursued by nameless enemies, but I was afraid to imagine their possible meaning, if they had any meaning at all. "Divina," I would say, "sometimes in the morning I can't move for hours." Knowing my condition better now, this length of time was impossible. I excused my own deficiencies because my father said he experienced the same thing: an odd dream paralysis state. All this simply provided an excuse for morning laziness, for which I was grateful. *Anything to avoid the sight of Binyamin.* I also dreamed of the future, my own role in the Gulf, one that seemed absurd: that I would be the conqueror of this system that had taken my mother and that I could be a leader in this confused place.

Through the Lord's help what was left of our family slowly recovered from our loss. Our dinner conversations grew and piece by piece we put together the puzzle of our bereavement. Slowly, we turned to daily events – school, wayward playmates, even Kuwaiti politics. I couldn't have managed without Divina's help. She was a constant source of consolation and order in our home, making sure that we were nurtured and offering stability when we felt rudderless and lost.

Over the years, I kept thinking and rethinking my mother's particular, even peculiar and frequent references to the book of Romans. She would say, "And we know that for those who love God all things work together for good, for those who are called according to his purpose" (Romans 8:28): This verse was a recurrent stumbling block for me. *How could this be true? How could her death work for our good?* I came to see I couldn't know the answers to these questions. I eventually realized the only course was to trust the goodness of God. Even so, I kept thinking of "my" purpose, not His.

We settled with the absence of my mother to the best extent possible. But I would never be the same without her. She had been the joy of my life, and that joy was gone. Now there was no one to guide me well as a Christian, and my spiritual growth remained stunted.

Mama had filled our home, not with the physical trappings of life which were ample, but with life from a spiritual source, one I had not yet incorporated. But I recognized its absence. Before her death she had forced me, yes, literally forced me, to complete the memorization of the entire book of Psalms. She afforded me no escape from the task. She was easy with Hibah but not with me. I think she knew my need for the Psalms would be greater than

Hibah's. Even though I viewed the book of Psalms as a plague, the Lord faithfully preserved His Word in my mind. However, it would be a long time before it came to fruition in my heart, and never as a finished work, not in this life.

As mentioned before, I was also gifted athletically, particularly in soccer. As I grew older, I was praised often by a larger group. My stride was long and smooth, and I thought I was superb at the sport. But my God-given insight lagged.

My success in academics and sports continued – team leadership and many goals. The experience confirmed what my father told me, and I saw myself through his eyes, captivated by his praise. Of course, I believed him, "Yusef, you're going to be amazing. You're so graceful on the pitch." Surely I'd be a professional soccer player. Soccer was like everything else in my young life: successful. But the truth was that I really wasn't that good at the sport.

Following my self-proclaimed success in schoolyard soccer I moved on to consider what lay beyond high school. My mother would have said I was reaching beyond what the Lord intended. Maybe I should have been content to just stay home and attend Kuwait University like Hibah.

Along the way there was another blessing. Binyamin announced

16

his personality, which was vibrant and outgoing, more than any of the rest of us. Despite our earlier, frank distaste for the little guy, he blossomed anyway, thanks to the love of Divina. By the age of five he searched my high school math books for problems. *Was he a genius?* Whenever I sat on the couch, he was there, on my lap, and I couldn't resist him.

By age sixteen, my default posture was one of prideful superiority as I waited for everyone to catch up with my ambition and plans for the future. I couldn't wait to draw the geographic and economic map of my future. Strange for an adolescent, but there it was. My hope to defeat those religious fanatics that had assaulted my mother's body after her death still preyed on my young mind. My juvenile solution was money: *Where would I have the greatest chance for financial success?*

What was the answer to my fervent question? My analysis, and I far exceeded my peers in such investigations, indicated to me it would not be on the western side of the Gulf.

CHAPTER 2

I LEARN OF ESAU

In May 2005 a Kuwaiti court sentenced twenty people to jail for having links to al-Qaeda. In September Mahmoud Ahmadinejad, Ayatollah Ali Khamenei, supporter and conservative hard-liner, won a landslide victory in Iran's presidential election. The Middle East was a jumble, and despite my brittle youthfulness, I looked to the future.

But the nearby grabbed prominence.

In the fall of 2006 I was sixteen when he took his job as new headmaster of the Kuwait English School. His name was Esau Allison, or Dr. Allison. On the morning of his first day, I heard the loudspeaker summons, "Yusef Al-Tamimi, report to the Headmaster's office." No one else was asked to report among the 600 students in our school. I knew enough Bible stories to be put off by the name Esau, and no one ever went to any headmaster's office for a good reason. As I left my first period calculus class, my mind was a muddle of possibilities: a bad grade of which I wasn't yet aware, *surely a mistake*, perhaps my standardized tests scores had fallen, *quite unlikely*, or some personal misstep, *surely not*.

The bespectacled secretary, an Indian woman with no head covering, told me to knock and enter his office. The window of the door was opaque, obscuring my view. Shaking and hoping it was not evident, I entered, disappointed by my own gloomy outlook. Sweat trickled down my back. Dr. Allison had his chair turned away from the door and toward the window and the light of the schoolyard with its white stone wall, marking the boundary. His chair creaked as he turned to face me, and placed his hairy hands palms down on his desk. His red hair and muscular forearms surprised me. Esau's biblical description immediately popped into my mind. He swung his large frame toward me and leaned forward at the waist, bringing his face as close to mine as the desk allowed. His lips were formed into a tight line, definitely not turned up at the corners in a smile. He didn't invite me to sit while he looked me up and down, a disconcerting welcome. He wore a dress suit, no dishdasha. *Another American here in our country for our money*, I thought. That should be no problem for me.

Surprisingly he spoke Arabic well. "So you're Yusef Al-Tamimi, son of Yacoub Al-Tamimi. Now I know what you look like. I see from your record you're doing very well here at my school." *Already, his school*. He smiled slightly. "For now," he stopped, letting that threatening phrase sink in, and then continued, "Well, never mind. Please return to your class." I focused on a bottle on his desk – the label said "sertraline." He picked it up, put it in the upper drawer of his desk, and locked it with a key. Turning his chair back to the window, he spoke no more.

Was I really dismissed? Just like that? How odd. Relieved but puzzled, I went back to class. Perhaps the doctor simply wanted to meet the better students and put faces to their names, so all day I expected others among the better students to be called to the office too. I was the best, and it was natural I would be asked first. But the day passed and no more names were announced.

Over dinner I began, "Papa, I met the new headmaster today. But it was strange. He didn't seem polite, or perhaps he didn't like me. His name is odd for an American: Esau, Esau Allison."

My father put down his fork (we now ate like the English) and didn't look at me; his color paled from its rich brown. "I know him, but it's not your concern. Did he have a Quran on his desk?"

He did, but so did a number of the faculty. That observation had no significance for me.

My father retired to his study without displaying his usual interest in my school day that night. I saw him open the side drawer of his oak desk and pull out a stack of rubber-banded letters with yellowed, frayed envelopes. Holding them in his hand, he glanced up at me and hastened to close the door. *What did this mean?*

The next day, I saw my father walk up the gravel pathway into the school grounds and enter the Headmaster's office in the break between my calculus and economics classes. I hurried to speak to him but he walked faster and turned away, avoiding me. *Why?*

21

Before I could reach him, he was in the office. After class, I saw my father's black Mercedes spin up gravel as he departed. He usually drove with more care. Their meeting had apparently required the full hour. My father had never bothered to come to my school on other occasions. In view of my academic status, there was no need, so that evening I challenged my father.

"Why did you go see Dr. Allison?"

My father was short with me, but certainly it was my business. *Why, Father?* "I've spoken with Esau. I think I've secured the means so he won't trouble you further. This is not your concern." That's all he would say to my persistent questions. *Why did he use the headmaster's first name: Esau?* Dr. Allison had not really troubled me, so I had no reason to expect otherwise, but I didn't like my father's tone. He knew more than he was sharing. I did not like being shut out. I was not a child, and it was my school. *How odd it is that teens think of themselves as adults. How is it that, in looking back when you thought you were a man, you realize in later years you weren't?*

I soon got to see more of Dr. Allison. As a computer expert with a PhD in computer science from Stanford, he took over as instructor for my computer class. He allowed me to flourish for the first month, and even permitted me to teach the lesson several times. Then came the assignment to write a simple program using Visual Basic.NET. I finished long before the others, those who could manage it at all. The assignment was too advanced for the class, and I suspected he had given it to shame us. I leaned back in my seat, waiting for the others to give up, arms folded, smug and self-important in my bearing. Dr. Allison looked directly at me while the others worked, smiled vaguely, and made several keystrokes. Suddenly, my computer screen began flashing with error messages.

"Yusef, please come to the front of the class and stand by my desk." He rose, stood by my side, and put his hand on my shoulder – his touch made me shiver. "Students, you see here in front of you a young man who believes he's better than you, but he only succeeds by cheating." I looked up at him. My mouth hung open, and my stomach contracted. "The program he just produced is an exact copy of one already written, which means he stole someone else's work. I just found his work in one of my old books. I can show you the two identical programs on the class screen."

Two programs popped up side by side on the class screen. The classroom erupted with scattered moans and nervous laughter. *But I had not copied the program. How had this man done this to me with such efficiency?* In retrospect I shouldn't have been so amazed.

"Students, in your handbooks you've seen the penalty for cheating, in this case blatant plagiarism. Immediate suspension. Mr. Al-Tamimi, get your things. I will phone your father to come and fetch you."

The shocked students stared, doubting my excellence for the first time, startled that the one they thought excellent was really a disgraceful fraud. A few looked confused. They had known me for a long time. Used to my arrogant manner, they now wondered.

It was clear to me though that I had been tricked, and my face tingled with fear or anger, I wasn't sure which. I had not cheated or plagiarized. The doctor's act was intentional and, for reasons I didn't know, vindictive. I gathered my books and computer and left the classroom, slamming the door behind me as hard as I could. The classroom computer screen shook with the jolt. There was no benefit now in showing respect.

I went straight to the Headmaster's office. The diminutive secretary tried to stop me but I brushed past her into the inner office, sat down, plopped my books on the floor, and waited.

Thirty minutes later Dr. Allison appeared, and I stood to confront him. I had nothing to lose, so I exploded. "Why did you do this? You know I didn't cheat. You made up the whole thing. I know you and my father know each other. If it's between you two, that's fine. Just leave me out of it. It's just not fair." I couldn't believe I said that to him, and the effort exhausted me.

At first he showed no emotion, but then his body stiffened and he pointed his finger directly in my face. I loathed his hairy hand. "Sit down, Yusef. I've won this round. Did you father tell you nothing? Typical. It's time for you to hear the truth."

I folded up in the chair like a deflated balloon while he stood. "When you get home — yes, I've phoned your father to come for you — you can ask your father to explain more, but he will lie. I am sure of it. I'm going to tell you the truth. We have the same father. Yes, you and I are brothers, half-brothers. Our father took advantage of my mother when he was her grad student. You might call it an affair. The affair ruined her marriage and left us without support. How we struggled after her husband left us." His eyes were red and bulging, and he used his height and girth to advantage. "Our father sent my mother pittances to support me but never enough. Worst of all, he never acted as my father. I was his secret. Well, I'm no longer a secret, am I? A debt has accrued over the forty-four years of my life. That's one part of this, and the other is this: you and your family are Christians; at least that's what you claim. You left Islam. We did not."

"I never left Islam. My mother and father raised me a Christian."

"The result is the same. You were born a Muslim, as are we all, but your family left Islam. I recognized I was a Muslim after my mother explained how Christians treated us. She made her point when she changed my name to Esau, a name of which I'm proud." *Suddenly, I felt afraid.* "You wonder why I'm in Kuwait? My mother's dead now, but I'm here to correct the wrongs against my mother and me and against Islam. There you have it. That's all you need to know, and I suggest you do not disclose our family connection with any of your classmates after you leave. If you do, it'll be even worse for you. I don't want to be related to my father, but I do want my revenge."

My father arrived shortly after Esau's speech. The eyes of my former classmates followed me out to the car as they changed classes. "Papa, is it true?" He didn't answer my question. His lack of denial was a confirmation.

"I have to tell you it's not going to end here. He's after all the Al-Tamimis, and he knew how to get at me through you. He is not finished yet," was my father's only statement.

###

He was right. That was only the beginning. My father said Esau was in Kuwait to dog us as Christians, and the meetings with our small gathering of believers had to be abandoned. "He'll lead the secret police to our meetings."

For the next two months I remained at home in Ahmadi. *What was worse? My father's initial failure to reveal what must have occurred in his university days? Or the boredom and pain in not being where I excelled?* I could only look out at the oil wells in the field near us, the ones that had made us rich. I used the time to read about the finances of Kuwait and the Gulf States, perhaps an odd hobby for a teenaged boy, but I loved the analysis required. *I would rise above this setback.*

Then, in the *Kuwait Times* an announcement appeared that Dr. Esau Allison had been named a vice-president of the Al Ahli Bank of Kuwait. "Papa, did you see this?" I asked, excited, "Surely now I can return to school." I was sick of our white stone house out in the Ahmadi desert, surrounded by the oil wells. The rhythm of the pumping wells was tedious.

My father's expression didn't change. He knew. "Yes, I've already arranged it." *My exile was over!* My father's enduring connections had helped get me back into school.

"However," he added thoughtfully, "in Esau's new position things will only get worse for us, the Tamimis and all the new Kuwaiti Christians. If he gets deep into the banking system, and it appears he's managed this, he can control many aspects of our lives. He hates us, and the only reason he's here is to get revenge. With his computer abilities, he'll try to find the identities of the secret Christians among us too. Even now, we can't worship freely. He's death to us."

Would I, would we all, have to fight this Esau forever? One day I might have to defend my family against this man and all he stands for. I decided then and there, when the time came, I would be ready. But ready for what?

.

CHAPTER 3

THE CHURCH GROWS AND TROUBLES BEGIN

Though there were Kuwaiti Christians, we had no church. We tried to be invisible, yet faithful. Since my father had stopped the informal gatherings for fear of Esau, we were now so hidden we barely knew each other, but my father sought a formula to move forward, and I joined to the extent I was able.

If my mother had lived during our desultory, early efforts at worshipping Jesus, our family would have handled every part of it with greater skill and hardier faith. But she was dead and we muddled through those early days to the best of our ability. She would have helped us see the Lord's hand in what occurred. My memories of her served me over the following years, but I was clumsy in faith, still not truly dedicated. Esau hung over us like a sword.

Since my mother passed away, my father had slowly gained in his walk with the Lord. At first he had begun leading us in prayer and reading the Word a bit during the week. I obliged.

Then my father reached a point of decision and invited his old friend, John Friedecker, over for tea. Yes, the Brits had left their refreshment remnants among us too and we enjoyed teatime. Friedecker pulled into the driveway and through our automatic, bronze gate in his old yellow Pajero, muffler rumbling and burning oil smell accompanying. Sometimes he wore the typical gray Kuwaiti dishdasha, the proper color for this time of the year, and he did so on this occasion. His beard was full and white, and his Caucasian skin crinkled with its long exposure to the desert sun. He had lived in Kuwait for more than twenty years as a history professor at Kuwait University, and was well-acculturated. We speculated that in the past he had been a secret missionary, but without obvious or known fruit for so many years, that description was difficult to sustain. Even so, he was in touch with the church in Kuwait.

We settled in our living room with the glass sliding door opening into the garden. It was late October and the daytime temperature had dropped from 120 degrees to the high 70s. Still a teenager, I smiled, proud at the privilege of my participation in the adult conversation. Hibah was there too, scowling, staring at my unworthy presence, taking her standard sister pose. I clasped my fingers together and waited, trying to appear as mature as possible. Given my recent experience as a Christian who had been attacked, I sat up straight, shoulders back, ready to participate. Binyamin was there too, hopping from one lap to another. He evoked cheer everywhere he was.

"John, what are we to do? We don't even know how to worship

properly." My father rose, pacing rather than sitting, hands on hips.

"I can't tell you what to do. You'll have to work it out for yourselves. There are others, former Muslims, here in Kuwait who're in the same circumstance," answered Friedecker, deadpan, not a sign of hope.

"Who are they? I want to get together with them."

"It's not time yet, Yacoub. It would be dangerous for us all."

"We need to worship Jesus, but, under the present circumstances, we don't know how. You have to tell us." He finally took his seat.

"Do what's in your heart. Decide what's best for your family. Rabea carried on in this spiritual hinterland for years before you were converted. She taught the Scriptures to Hibah and Yusef."

My father looked down and shook his head. "I don't know where to start. I'm not even sure I know the correct name for God. In America, Christians were offended when I said 'Allah.'"

"That's easy to deal with. Allah has been used by Middle Eastern Christians for centuries as the word for God. It's close to the Hebrew *Elohim,* so it works. There are harder questions for you to handle. Should you go to the NECK (National Evangelical Church of Kuwait) down by the Gulf?" *My mother had gone to the NECK once, and they had asked her not to return.*

"Rabea said they didn't really want new Kuwaiti Christians

31

there. The government might shut them down for proselytizing."

"Perhaps the NECK will not work for your family then. It might be dangerous for you and probably that church too. Is that church what Christianity looks like for you? You could go to the mosque to worship Jesus. There are those who were formerly Muslims but are now Christians who attend the mosque. We call them MBBs or Muslim background believers." *Another mystery. No clarity here for me.*

"Who is 'we'?"

"Never mind that."

"I haven't been to mosque regularly for years." Papa went occasionally for show.

"Maybe you should see how it feels now. See if you could worship there."

We were already frightened what Esau might do to us in his new position, and now we were going to go to the mosque. Any sense of confidence among us disappeared: Hibah paled and her nervous cough punctuated the afternoon. This collection of events baffled me.

But all at once, Hibah, reedy and thin like my mother, echoed what I thought my mother would have said, had she lived. In a moment, she shook off her fears, gathered herself to an erect posture, and held up her right hand as if in a benediction, an odd posture even for her. "There's no need to be afraid. The Lord brought us this far, and He'll get us the rest of the way. I don't want to go to the mosque, but where else could we begin again?" She was the image of my mother, and her lack of startling beauty was overcome by her grace and methodical approach.

The next Friday we went to the mosque in Ahmadi. Its two light blue minarets mocked us as we approached. The usual large Friday crowd was in the process of entering. Hibah, my father, and I entered through the gender-specific doors.

It was an ongoing challenge for us to separate the components of Islamic worship practices into those we thought permissible for believers in Jesus and those that were clearly outside that realm. The ritual washing or cleansing was the first concern. Hibah told me she would forego the washing. I washed in the prescribed fashion, called *wudu* in Arabic, splashing the hands, mouth, nostrils, arms, head and feet with water. I must have looked awkward and uncertain. The water was not intended for hygienic cleanliness but for spiritual purity. I was in need of such cleansing, that was true, but I knew this did nothing to cleanse my true spiritual state. I hoped the women had not noticed Hibah's neglect of the washing. For me, however, the water cooled and refreshed my skin.

None of us were troubled by the imam's sermon dealing with the necessity for kind treatment of the Third World nationals who worked in Kuwait. His instruction was oriented solely to encourage our good behavior. Everyone knew it was for show, maybe for the newspaper reporters in the congregation.

33

Going through the *salat* (a complex prayer) as we stood in rows was more intellectually challenging. I was stiff and unsure of myself, but I'm sure Hibah managed the subtleties with greater ease than my father or me. Facing Mecca did not have any particular significance for me so I joined in this action. I easily recited the first chapter of the Quran: "In the name of Allah, Most Gracious, Most Merciful. Praise be to Allah, Lord of the Worlds. Most Gracious, Most Merciful, Master of the Day of Judgment. Thee alone we worship and Thee alone we ask for help. Show us the straight path. The path of those whom Thou hast favored; not the path of those who earn your anger nor of those who go astray," directing these thoughts to God in my mind. The second passage: "Say: He is Allah, the One! Allah is He on Whom all depend. He does not beget, nor is He begotten. And there is none like unto Him," also seemed benign enough to me, but Hibah reminded my father and me later that "He does not beget" was a direct negation of Jesus' role as deity because it denied the statement of John 3:16 regarding Jesus as God's "only son." Saying, "Glory be to my Lord, the Almighty" and "Glory be to my Lord, the most High" were clear and certainly my own praise. The last portion of the prayer raising praise to Mohammed as a prophet was definitely out of bounds. My lips were silent. At the end, we turned our faces to the right and the left, conferring God's peace on those around us, "Peace be upon you and the mercy of Allah."

We emerged, exhausted and sweating from the brief service. Our attempts to remain true to Jesus and still not be obvious in the mosque were conflicting. Hibah's face was drawn and unhappy. My father hung his head. Could we do this again? At best, it was unsatisfying. At worst, it invalidated what Jesus had done for us. On some level, I envied the other worshippers who were relaxed, talking easily among themselves, certain of their place, and happy at the rapid conclusion of the service. Would we continue the mosque charade? Surely there must be something better for us.

My father told John of our experience and feelings, and, as usual, he was unsympathetic. He had long experience with the compromises Christians in a Muslim country had to make to survive. There were few options.

We persisted in attendance for the next ten weeks. Our friends in the Ahmadi community were glad to see that we were coming to the more often. We tolerated the experience by retreating from the externals of the service and making worship an intimate transaction between the Lord and ourselves, silent and unbetrayed by our actions. Still, we knew in our hearts that worship should be a celebration of Christ's life, an event to be experienced with other believers. We did not have this privilege, and knew that if we tried to pursue a real, community experience at this time, the secret police would soon know and intervene. We were not prepared for that.

Esau also attended the mosque for Friday prayers. When he saw us, he approached us straightaway, as if he planned to knock us over with a blow. We sidestepped him, but not before he uttered "liars" as he drew near. We simply got in our car. As we drove off, he stood gazing at us, hands extended and palms up, as if to say: *Why are you here?*

It was more than a month before I even looked around at the mosque to acquaint myself with others who attended. Dhuwaihi, who had been a participant in my father's dīwāniya (a men's discussion group) was always present. He was an old man, and his appearance betrayed his failing health – he was short of breath and coughed through the service.

I noticed that his actions at the Friday prayers were unusual. He skipped the ritual washing. During prayer he stopped the repetition in the portions that referred to the prophetic stature of Mohammed. I wondered if he was a kindred spirit, but he avoided us by retreating if we came near. Finally, during the next service my father maneuvered his way to pray next to him, and they spoke after the service. "May the peace of Allah be with you, Yacoub and Yusef." He was stiff, unusually reserved, and there was no other exchange. This process continued for weeks, but eventually it became clear he was seeking us out during the service too. He watched our every move as we participated.

After another month, he stopped us in a private place among the large columns of the tan marble portico outside the mosque after the service. Each column was large enough to obscure three men talking together. "I've been watching you, and I've observed there are certain, well, let's say deficiencies in your worship. Is this accidental or due to a lack of diligence?"

My father replied, "It's no accident. I've observed you display the same tendencies. I've begun to think these behaviors are consistent with a certain alternate viewpoint." They looked at one another, neither party wishing to go further.

Peering closely at us, Dhuwaihi finally spoke, "Yes, indeed they are. There are others with the same viewpoint too. Perhaps you both could come to my home for further talk. This afternoon?"

But we when we arrived at Dhuwaihi's modest home, there were no other cars or visitors. Our expectation of meeting other Kuwaiti Christians was wiped out. Dhuwaihi's house was small by well-to-do Kuwaiti standards: one story with a low wall at the front entry area, no automatic gate, no attendant. He ushered us into his living room: The creaky furniture was dusty, cracked, and uncomfortable. Old photographs hung on the walls, hearkening from the days when Kuwait was just dust and sand. The home betrayed an old man who was lonely, or at least estranged from others.

My father asked, "Why are no others here?" I noticed he had a small black dog that followed him closely. Owning a dog was unusual for traditional Arabs.

Dhuwaihi answered, "It's too dangerous for us to meet together as believers. We avoid any of us knowing the names of the others. You should know there is a new threat. His name is Esau Allison, and he's an executive at the Al Ahli Bank." My father nodded. "We think he's collecting a list of Kuwaiti Christians. What he intends to do with that list once he has it, we don't know. We think he's intercepting Internet communications. He has connec-

tions with strict Wahhabi groups. You know about the Wahhabis."
I knew little, and made a mental note to learn more. "Esau's on a mission,"Duwaihi finished.

My father and I glanced at each other briefly. "Thank you for warning us about him," my father remarked. "I don't know what we can do to counter him, but I do think we as Christians need to build one another up in our faith, in any way we can. I'll give some thought to that at any rate."

Dhuwaihi nodded and made us tea.

It was several weeks later that Hibah told us to invite Dhuwaihi to join us for a meal after Friday mosque. The old man was essentially without close family, and that meant there was no danger of any complicated interaction with other family members. He accepted.

Dhuwaihi parked his car in the driveway. It was an old, dark blue Chevy Caprice, a vehicle with air conditioning that was known to manage the vicious Kuwaiti summers. The leather dashboard, split by years of high temperatures, had been replaced by a worn velvet covering. Once he arrived, we settled briefly in the sunlit room beside the pool, and Hibah called us for dinner. She and Divina had prepared lamb *machboos*, a dish with basmati rice and *kibbeh* (a mixture of bulgur, minced onions, and finely ground meat), preceded by the lentil soup, hummus and *khubz* (a round, leavened flatbread). Typical of Kuwaiti meals, the challenge was always to prepare more than the guest could ever eat. Dhuwaihi finished in the proper manner, leaving some on his plate. This sent the appropriate message: that there was more than enough. At the end of the meal, Binyamin crawled onto his lap and pulled Dhuwaihi's beard, not once, but twice. We all laughed along with Binyamin.

Accounts of our conversions filled the time. Dhuwaihi began. "I was an old man by the time I came to know Him. My family put me out. They thought me odd because I read all the time. And there were other reasons. I had to learn English in order to read the Old Testament. There were no Arabic translations of the Old Testament available in Kuwait at the time. Once I read it, I saw the story from beginning to end. And it is a story, not like the Quran. There was no way for me to avoid the conclusion that God was speaking to me. That was three years ago. I stopped smoking at that time because it was destroying the body Allah gave me, but it was too late. You've heard my cough. Like all our sins, even though they're forgiven, they still follow you. Eventually I began to meet others who know Jesus, but I've continued to go to the mosque, at least for the time being." It was a refreshing experience to exchange our beliefs freely. Even though my testimony seemed more superficial than the others, our words felt fresh and new. Dhuwaihi sat quietly, his chest rising and falling too fast, listening intently.

Hibah wept as she shared her story in which our deceased mother was the star. Then she asked, "Dhuwaihi, where is all this headed? What will become of new Arab believers here and elsewhere?

You've already indicated there are others." Hibah had left her hair uncovered in Dhuwaihi's presence.

"Allah knows. In that we must be comforted." His cough interrupted his remarks. "The change won't stop, but it won't be smooth or easy or without blood. I don't know where it's headed, but I do know you children are the key. Your mother taught you well."

Then, Dhuwaihi assumed a different tone and used his age as a pedestal. "Hibah, you're a joy. You're beautiful, wonderfully confident. But Yusef, you shock me. You're not like a teenage boy. There's something else I can't identify. It's beyond being handsome. Your demeanor is like that of a man of achievement." He stopped for nearly a full minute. "But you've achieved nothing, and I'm afraid I see trouble in you. No, that's not exactly right. But for certain – difficulty. Perhaps the answers to the questions we're asking are in you. I know that sounds strange."

The afternoon was spent. The sun came directly from the window into our eyes and we turned away from the glare. *Did Dhuwaihi intend this as a prophecy about me?* He didn't identify it as such, but the tone of the comment set it aside from the rest of the conversation. *What did he mean by it? In some ways, his pronouncement reminded me of my mother and the way she saw right into me, but it went beyond that. How could solutions be found in me? I had no idea.*

###

Two weeks later, Dhuwaihi was missing from the mosque. He had not been absent for months, and we hoped the old man was not ill. As we got to our car, Abdullah Al-Bader came hurrying up to my father. "I have sad news. I can't imagine why this has happened. You know Dhuwaihi, the old man. The bank is going to take his house! On top of that, his family doesn't want him back. He's a bit strange, but don't you think his family should help him? He will have nowhere to live!"

We drove home quickly. My father was distressed as were the rest of us. "How can this happen? Dhuwaihi's not rich, but he's been careful with his money. He chose a modest house for that reason."

My father phoned Dhuwaihi. "We heard about the house. What happened?"

"I don't know what happened. I received a letter from the bank, demanding that I pay 50,000 dinars or they'll take my home. I asked a lawyer from the city center to look at the letter, and he says it's perfectly legal. The bank says my home is no longer worth enough to secure the value of the loan. According to an old law on the books, this new valuation of my house allows the bank to demand the money. No one's ever heard of this law being used before."

Dhuwaihi was ruined. Since his family wouldn't take him in, he would be without a place to live. It was unheard of for a Kuwaiti to be homeless. This couldn't happen.

My father thought he might be able to help. "What bank is it?"

"The Al Ahli Bank."

My father, Hibah, and I drove over to see Dhuwaihi, partly to console him and partly to look at the letter. Dhuwaihi, the furrows in his face deeper than ever, handed it to my father. After a quick look, my father shook his head, looked down and uttered a phrase he never used, *"Al-Sheitan Alaykom!* (Satan be upon you!)" He passed the letter to Hibah and I looked at it over her shoulder. "Look at the signature," he said. At the bottom was the name Esau Allison, with the words Chief Loan Officer under it. Hibah, already in law school, inspected the paperwork and was at a loss as to how to proceed.

Was it because Dhuwaihi was a Christian? How had Esau even found out that he was a Christian? The only likely answer was through the Internet. The old man had indeed adopted this modern form of communication. From my own experience, I knew that Esau excelled in this area, and he clearly intended to use his skills and financial means to attack Christians.

The old man's home was preserved only by the joint action of several believers, so far unknown to us by name, who stepped in and paid the debt. The fact that these Christians assisted as they did indicated Dhuwaihi's circle of believers was larger than we suspected. My father contributed 10,000 dinars. The good part was that Esau had no idea who helped Dhuwaihi; and in the end, Esau's actions only bolstered the unity of the secret community.

As a result, my own resolve strengthened. For me, Esau now embodied all the enemies of Christians. He was the bull's eye of my target. *How could a young person like me be the equal of a capable, middle-aged man?* There would come a time for more action, if not just by me, but from all my family.

###

My choice was to proceed with the gifts God gave me, relying on them as though they were mine to possess. I had already been informed of my charm, too much so, but Esau had been impervious to my charms; only his own counted for him. Since finances were to be the battleground, I decided to develop my skills in that area. I was sure they would get me to my goal, whatever that might be. Where would this take me? Surely, not just Kuwait. Esau was only the current representative of the enemy. Would his influence spread beyond Kuwait? I needed to prepare for that if they did.

And what's more, Gulf fortunes were rising higher elsewhere than those in little Kuwait. *I remembered my old dream of being king of the Gulf.*

CHAPTER 4

WHAT I THOUGHT OF THE GULF

Hibah did not go along with me. "You can't just leave us and go wandering off to college across the world. We have to fight Esau and his kind, and we need you here in Kuwait to do it. There's nothing wrong with Kuwait University." She was right; there wasn't. Hibah flashed her black eyes at me, but it was only a glancing blow.

"You don't know where the clash with Esau will lead. This is a lot bigger than Kuwait. I'm going where I can find the best prospects."

She stormed out of the room, elbows flailing like chicken wings. Then she turned, put her hands on her thin hips, and said tearfully, "Our mother's gone, and Papa needs you here."

In the fall of 2008 as I prepared to apply for university, a bitter fight took shape between me and my father and Hibah. Papa tried to step in where my mother would have spoken out. "Yusef, we want you to stay with us here in Kuwait. I left when I finished high school, and I paid the price for years. Esau being in our lives

45

today shows that we're still paying the price. Hibah's right. We need you here for all that's coming." Our home, for the time, was a battleground: me against them.

But I was nearly eighteen, the age of "always right"; I knew my future lay outside Kuwait. The world was changing fast. Barack Obama had gained the democratic nomination for U.S. president. "Papa, little Kuwait has nothing in its favor beyond the oil still in the ground. I know the country has invested all over the world as a plan against the end of oil, but that doesn't do the average Kuwaiti any good. Nobody ever talks about anything but the oil, but other things will overwhelm us if we don't get involved."

Why would I even consider leaving my family in Kuwait and heading off on a grand search? I was fascinated with the future and what my role would be in it. As the center of my concerns, I crafted a view I thought was consistent with the ongoing conflicts I read about in the Gulf.

Often, I argued and ruined another meal. "Look what's happened just since I was born. Even after the Iraqis were thrown out of Kuwait in 1991, they tried to come back. I was only a toddler but I remember you talking about their attacks two years after the war, when they came across our border in little sorties, just to test what we would do. We didn't do anything." I stood and my father sat, his arms resting on the chair, on doilies placed there by my mom. "The Iraqis tested our will, and they found none. They tried the will of the U.S. to come again to our defense, and thank the Lord, the Americans fended off the invaders again. Doesn't that tell you how weak we are? The Americans didn't do it for us though. They did it for the oil."

My father looked down, unsmiling, but surely he knew it was true. Did it bring back memories for him of the 1990 Gulf War and his own flight from Kuwait to save himself? But I didn't care for his feelings. I was cruel, showing no regrets for rekindling the memories of his desertion.

My father had tried to insulate me from the petty political squabbles in Kuwait. "We're above all that nonsense of the fights between the monarchy and parliament," he would tell me. But it became apparent to me, even as a teenager, that our leaders were fighting over nothing of any real importance, and that the real issues were being addressed in other areas of the Persian Gulf, especially in Iran. The news and CNN confirmed my impressions. Unlike me, my schoolmates displayed little interest in the news. Why should they? We were children of privilege. Our future stretched before us like the steady flow of the oil that was the guarantee of our wealth. We could depend upon it. Oil or no, I reveled in the notion that I could see the events of a much larger area together and conceive a better scheme. My dreams played in my mind like a constant drumbeat.

"I know exactly what I'm doing. Kuwait is not going to be the major player in the times to come," I said to my family in yet another tense conversation. Such was my only reflection.

Hibah did not agree. "You don't know that, Yusef. Look at the progress women have made. We have been allowed to vote now for several years, and even run for parliament. How can you insinuate there is no possibility for success and no real future here in Kuwait? I think I may run for parliament myself as soon as I'm able."

"Hibah, women have never won any seats in parliament. Take Massouma Al-Mubarak. She's been active in politics for a long time, and can't win a seat." I was on a roll. "She's argued for women's rights for years. She messed up her chances for any election when she collected signatures for a petition opposing gender segregation in education. The Emir threw a bone to women when he appointed her the first female cabinet officer, but it was all political trickery. Massouma knew it and so should you. That doesn't mean Kuwait is at the forefront of anything.

"Papa, remember when Jaber died and Sheik Saad was inserted in his place?" I countered quickly, not restraining myself from my thoughtless harangue. "You know how soon Saad was removed because of his obvious deficiencies. It was just a family plot. Sheikh Sabah became Emir and did all he could to keep his whole family in power. It's always like that here." The evening sun faded into the sand, an orange sunset resulting. "They did everything to assure the continuity of their own family. They guaranteed Kuwait wouldn't change." What I didn't say was that I admired the Sabah's aggressive consolidation of power.

By this time, I was so enamored with my own understanding of the intricacies of Kuwaiti politics, that I could not help but continue my adolescent invective. "Everything in Kuwaiti politics centers on the Sabah family. The Sabahs manipulate the elec-

48

tions, and then when they're accused, they blame someone else. How long can they maintain this level of control? No one said a peep when Kuwaitis were told to conserve electricity in order to support the financial income generated by the oil. Did the average Kuwaiti see any of the additional income produced by this maneuver? No."

"And look at Iran. It was only a year ago when they succeeded in enriching uranium at the Natanz facility. The UN's deadline for Iran halting work on nuclear fuel passed with Iran continuing its progress anyway! The International Atomic Energy Agency just admitted Iran could develop a nuclear weapon within a few years. They are pulling way ahead of us."

Recently, *Al-Jazeera* had been prominent as the recent Qatari addition to the news media, and I read its Internet pages with relish. In them, I saw opportunities unfolding, not here in Kuwait but across the Persian Gulf in Iran. They beckoned me. I told myself that since Esau was confined to Kuwait, I would be free to operate against his influence if I were in Iran. Looking back on this conversation, I realize that my vocabulary and knowledge of the international news sounded odd for a teenager, but I know now how childish and selfish my thoughts really were. I knew the jargon of politics, but little else, and I distorted the facts to support my views. What did I really know?

By this time Hibah was quite upset, not only about my plan to leave, but also about my hammering away on our father. I pressed on. As I reflect on this now, I'm ashamed, but I had stubbornly continued then. "What happened the last time the Emir canned

49

parliament? Do you remember? After the call for new elections, the radicals made gains, winning more than half the fifty seats. Hibah, were any women elected? No, of course not." Hibah was cowed and tearful, a posture uncommon for her. "Now we're left with a political situation that is rapidly turning into a conflict between the liberals and religious extremists. The only real victory for women was a ruling to allow women to obtain passports without consent of their husbands. How ridiculous does that sound? These small-time politicians are sapping our country's strength and any competitive edge we could hope to achieve. Kuwait is weak and engaged only in its own self-interest." My father didn't counter. Perhaps he saw he was wasting his time in arguing with me. I was heartless to even keep it up. After all, I was going to do what I was going to do anyway and everyone knew it now.

"Look at what's going on in other Gulf States. They're all moving faster and in a more modern direction then we are. Little Qatar is just an example. The Qataris are allowing a new Christian church to be built. Soon they'll outstrip us in the freedoms we offer and in the potential wealth that dribbles down to their citizens." Qatar had become one of the two biggest shareholders in the London Stock Exchange. The Gulf area was awash in change and my visualization of the events propped up my ego. As if I needed that.

I viewed all these events as possible advantages to me. I anticipated a great future for myself, and consequently saw the importance of becoming politically engaged, but I planned to do this in a novel way. The answer would lie in the flow of money and the ability of one, namely me, to act upon that tide. I wanted what I wanted.

The real puzzle, however, was Iran where not only were there vast oil reserves but also untapped intellectual wealth and more diversity than ever recognized by most of the world. I read of these events from as many sources as I could get my hands on. Our Kuwaiti news sources remained shallow, self-focused, incomplete, and uninterested in Iran.

I launched into more of my newfound knowledge about Iran. To me as a teenager, it was as if I was the first to make these discoveries. Now I was lecturing my father and sister. "With all that's going on in Iran, their people still carry on with courage. They want their rights, much more than Kuwaitis." Divina avoided eye contact with me as she served tea.

Young Iranians continued to participate in anti-government protests. I thought the Iranian people were endowed with more courage than the Kuwaitis – another youthful, hopeful thought about a matter outside my experience.

The election of Ahmadinejad as president of Iran in 2005 came on top of the clumsy management of the U.S. invasion in Iraq. The U.S. withdrew its support from Iraq after ridding the country of Saddam Hussein. Their departure left a power vacuum, increasing the influence of Iran and Shia Islam in the Gulf, so the Shia majority in Iraq and Iran were inspired.

"You've seen the Iraqi Shia on TV celebrating in the streets. The shift in power in Iraq has enhanced the influence of Iran. The

U.S. is afraid of a nuclear-tipped Iran. They've increased sanctions but it's not helping. You'll see, Iran is going to be a major power. I'm sure of it, and I want to be there." I would get back at Esau through my own clever plan, one that did not center in Kuwait. No Esau in Iran.

The back-and-forth rhetoric and political activity in Iran indicated to me a widespread multiplicity of views, much more extreme than in the other Gulf States. Iran was a hothouse of competing ideas and trends. In 2003 Shirin Ebadi, an Iranian attorney and founder of the Defenders of Human Rights Center, was awarded the Nobel Peace Prize for her work as a judge favoring human rights. In 2008 Iranian police, presenting no warrant, raided and closed the office of her center. Officials said the center was acting as an illegal political organization. Later, she was forced to live in exile in Great Britain.

I therefore settled on Iran as my field of combat. There I would make my fortune and along with it, get the ammunition for the battle to achieve victory over Esau and the likes of him.

Victory, but victory over what? What was I really shooting for? Was it my personal financial goal? Could I make a contribution in Iran as a Christian? Yes, that was one of my hopes. In my anger toward Esau and how he had dogged my family, I put my future success in Iran together in the same basket with defeating Esau and all those who hated Christians. My youthful financial analysis supported my plan.

I had already made my choice about a university long before my argument with Papa and Hibah. There was no way I was staying in Kuwait. King's College in London was my first choice and I was confident my grades, TOFEL, and SAT scores were good enough to get in. Of course, they were. I anticipated I would find my entry card to Iran there.

My father had another son, my half-brother Thawab, from an earlier failed marriage. Thawab began visiting our home on Friday afternoons and meeting with small groups of men around this same time. I was not informed about their purpose, but I suspected it was more than social.

Again I dreamed about what would occur in the future, but I was afraid to tell anyone – it was too ridiculous and frightening.

As for my brother, perhaps my father was actually taking action. Thawab was forty-one, and I had no emotional connection to this half-brother nearly thirty years older than me. It seemed unbelievable that Thawab would play a role, but it was evident my father loved him, and I kept silent.

The pot churned in the Gulf and in little Kuwait. In January 2009 Sheik Nawaf had formed a new government following another disagreement in parliament. In the spring three women, including Massouma Al-Mubarak, finally won seats in parliament elections. Hibah couldn't resist. "See, Yacoub, there is a chance for us.

My occasional spells of spontaneous sleep during the day and my more frequent morning visions continued unabated. I often woke, unable to move while dreamlike images flashed in front of me. I failed to integrate them into any mental picture of my glorious future. Had I done so, I would have lived in fear and perhaps even abandoned my plan. Were the dreams I experienced like those of my biblical namesake? Look what he had endured!

My departure at the airport was enlivened only by Binyamin, who hugged my neck and refused to let go. I didn't want him to stop, and he buried his head between my head and shoulder. Hibah had refused to join the goodbyes.

When I left for London my father was seventy-one.

CHAPTER 5

KING'S COLLEGE

I made my way to London's King's College in the fall of 2009. I was determined to go there. Besides, it was only natural I would follow in my father's footsteps and attend there. Even though he was certain I should stay in Kuwait, I told him I had to go there, claiming that I wanted to follow the way he had gone, but I was really following my own will. I would not, however, seek a doctoral degree as he did. His investigation of Islamic law had led him into a morass from which he escaped only with God's help. I vowed not to follow the steps that led him astray; my own march turned out to be adequate for that purpose anyway.

Almost simultaneous with my enrollment at King's, Iran admitted they were building a nuclear enrichment facility near Qom, the Persian center of religious study. *Any irony there?* Their intentions looked belligerent in nature, and this was confirmed for the world by their test-firing a series of medium- and long-range ballistic missiles soon after. I watched the TV reports on CNN not knowing, but imagining, how these events would affect my future. *What an adventure faced me!* At least Esau had no involvement there.

The stairs creaked as I walked up the three flights to my dorm room. Having just arrived from Kuwait where it was boiling hot, I shivered as the cold rain dripped from my thin, brown leather jacket. Purchased in Kuwait, it did not prove waterproof. Each step bore a small puddle from an earlier arrival, and I fell and bruised my knee. I got out the key for the dorm room, but the door was unlocked and ajar. Both room windows were wide open. I shut them first thing and attempted to turn on the radiator, an ancient gray-painted device with which I was wholly unfamiliar. The gray monster clanged away when I succeeded. The room was cluttered with crumpled newspapers, empty soft drink bottles, and candy wrappers. How could my new roommate have created this mess so quickly? It was not Kuwaiti standard.

I dried off the best I could: we had one towel apiece on the rack in the room. At 2 a.m., my assigned roommate, Adam Farmson, arrived singing the tenor part from "Sweet Adeline" at the top of his voice. He had no talent for music.

By that time, I had picked up his trash. He greeted me with, "Thanks much, chum, for doing the maid service. So that's going to be your job here, eh? I've just had the first pub debauch of my previously pure life." The son of an Anglican pastor from Wales, he was free in London from his childhood moorings. "So, you're my Muslim roomie. I suppose that's why you couldn't go out to the pubs." He reopened the windows and turned off the radiator. Then he grabbed his stomach, bent over, and stumbled out to the hall bathroom, gurgling and smelling like sour apples. After retching, he came back to our room and collapsed onto his bed without getting under the covers.

I couldn't resist. "It appears you shouldn't have gone yourself."
He didn't hear me, and I heard nothing more from him except
snoring until morning.

"Was I unpleasant last night? I've never had more than one
drink a night. When I knew I didn't have to go home to father,
I got carried away. Listen chum, you don't have a chance here.
I assume English isn't your native language, and for that reason alone, you're fried." He talked at me over his shoulder as he
pulled off last night's vomit-stained socks. "And you're an Arab.
You guys are always in the news about some type of fighting and
killing, so the profs are going to shoot you down right from the
beginning. You'd better get your wardrobe adjusted. Also, my father, the preacher, would want me to talk to you about why you
shouldn't be a Muslim."

"Okay, you've convinced me. Now, I'm Christian," I answered.
Already, we didn't like each other.

He spun his head around and looked at me. "Don't make fun
of me. My father taught me about Muslims. Should I be afraid to
sleep in the same room with you?"

"No, I really am a Christian." I dispensed the required explanation, and finally he accepted my status as a believer. About his
status, I remained unconvinced, but we tacitly agreed to tolerate
each other as roommates after that.

###

My major concentration was international economics and finance with an emphasis on the Middle East. My knowledge of Middle East politics was superior to that of my schoolmates, and I used those skills to excel at King's. I dug into my classes and completed the basics with a 4.0: all As. The courses in finance dealt with material I had already covered in my reading before I came. As a result, my time in London was not devoted solely to study. I did, however, avoid the sexual misadventures of my father. I had no time for romance. With all the women sporting revealing dress, it was a challenge, but I emerged pure in this realm. Frankly, Western women frightened me.

Adam commented on my marks. "Did your rich family pay off the profs?"

After I had the basic principles of finance down, I was sure I had a safe bet for my Iran plan. The source of power in the Gulf was money, so my goal was knowing all the ins and outs of managing it well. Notwithstanding Saudi oil, I saw Iran as the real power base, the pivotal player in the Gulf, which meant my foreign language concentration had to be Farsi. All this, by my calculation, was pointed at the Esau fight. I didn't know how correct I was.

Accustomed to the role from my experiences in Kuwait, I starred in campus life. Thinking of Hibah, I joined the political action group on the rights of women. It was soon suggested that I run for class president.

My competitor was male, British, and white. I got most of the female vote and some of the men's. *Roar News*, the student paper, posted the headline: "Kuwaiti Yusef Al-Tamimi Elected Fresh-man Class President." Farmson was beside himself. Due to the ongoing news of strife in the Arab world and the growing negative impression of Arabs, I considered my selection as a singular achievement. The student union filled with my congratulators, and I bought coffees all round.

And then there was intramural soccer. I relished the afternoon when I heard the little group of onlookers shout, "Goal! Goal! Goal!" each of the three times I scored from the wing. My joy was enhanced when I saw the defeated expression of the opposing goalkeeper, Farmson.

I continued to experience dreams a few hours after going to sleep. Their content at this point was standard – pursuit by vicious foes, falling in space, failing to complete an assignment, and the like – nothing prophetic or symbolic. And then, more pointedly, or perhaps prophetically, came the Esau dreams. Why did he seek me out in dreams? Did the dreams foreshadow any real event?

Farmson baffled me. "I never have dreams," he said. This was not possible.

Adam resented my dreams because I sometimes made a commotion when I was sleeping. A hurled shoe often woke me. Less frequent were the morning dreams, if they should be called dreams, which occurred when I was in the phase between awake and asleep but unable to move.

My father had explained to me he had the same condition, which he called narcolepsy. I was thankful I didn't have the falling attacks that afflicted him. The morning visions I experienced while awake were frightening enough. Each time I was paralyzed. Every time they occurred, the foreboding they brought with them was new and fresh. For reasons I couldn't grasp, the assurance of eventual recovery eluded me during these visions. I learned they had a medical name: hypnogogic hallucinations. Knowing this made me question my sanity. Sometimes all I could see in the "dream" was a room with three white walls and bars on the fourth side. I could never see beyond it.

###

My father told about one of his favorite hangouts, the Red Lion Pub, and I became a regular there. With its red neon lion on the window, the pub was a small, darkly lit room, long and narrow in shape. There were high stools along the bar, uncomfortable for an Arab used to sitting on the floor, but along the opposite wall and extending to the back there were wooden booths with high backs, a good place for private conversation. I went there for fellowship, not the ale, at least not at first.

Colleagues at the Red Lion, knowing of my interest in Iran, suggested a Googoosh concert. Googoosh was a popular singer-entertainer in Iran prior to the 1979 revolution. She was little known in the Gulf, and her flamboyant style was not suitable to the ghost of the revolution, so from 1979 until 2000 she was not permitted to perform, living as an exile in her own land. In 2000 the newly elected President Mohammed Khatami gave her the gift to perform, but only abroad. The senselessness of this ruling didn't penetrate the minds of the authorities.

We took off from the pub in time to get tickets to her concert in the London theater district. Her purple, sequined dress was low in front and tightly cut, nothing like what I expected from a Middle Eastern woman. Heavy makeup obscured her years, and she sang in Farsi, her voice rich and husky. I was able to understand a few of the words. In one of her songs, called "I Want," she celebrated her tortured, difficult past, repeating the phrase, "born again" over and over. What did she mean by "born again"? Her words served as confirmation for me that the future of the Gulf lay in Iran. Even in her musical seniority, she breathed vitality.

The courses in Farsi offered at King's College were basic, as the language was unpopular in the West. Due to my native Arabic, I was already familiar with the writing and sounds signified by the script. In order to progress further, it was necessary for me to enter language immersion in Iran, which meant living with a Persian family for an extended period. It was not a simple matter for a Kuwaiti citizen to obtain a visa for a lengthy stay in Iran, but my father was able to arrange it. He was generous toward me, even though I had not followed his instruction to remain in Kuwait. With his help, I became an honored guest in Iran.

In 2009, in what should have been a warning to me, three

U.S. citizens out for a mountain hike in 2009 were arrested on the Iran-Iraq border, found guilty of spying and sentenced to eight years in prison. *No problem,* I thought, *I'm not a spy.*

Soon it was reported that Iran was carrying out research to develop a nuclear bomb trigger. Iran rejected the report as politically motivated. My classmates questioned my plan to study there. "Are you crazy going to that place? You'll probably get yourself arrested."

When I did go, I traveled first to the capital city of Tehran where I spent several days sightseeing. The Golestan Palace grounds housed a series of seventeen buildings, all arches and columns with blue reflecting pools, now used for social events as well as the National Museum. There was the Pond House, the Picture House, and the Museum of Gifts to name a few. While I thought Islamic art avoided painting and sculpture of natural objects and emphasized calligraphy and design, this was not the case for the palace. There were art pieces from many eras among the more standard designs. The sculptures were minimalist in their form, but clearly human. Why wouldn't the extremists say this was idolatry? Their deep culture had transcended that portion of the theocracy.

The cosmopolitan character of Tehran, despite the Islamic influence, startled me. I knew the people were not free but their street behavior was full of laughter, black leather jackets, and smiling women, hair covered but some arrayed with bright colors. The music blasting out to the street from the shops pounded my eardrums. An upscale dress shop played "I Gotta Feeling" by the Black-Eyed Peas.

Not all the women were freely dressed. The chador is a black, full-length robe open in front like a coat, and covering all or part of the face. Its purpose is to conceal the female form. What a sad thought! Two chador-covered women brushed hard against me even though there was ample space on the sidewalk, and youthful giggles came from under their black façades. One turned and looked back. Was she smiling? Her outfit obscured that information. I would never know.

A Persian proverb says, *"Esfahān nesf-e- jahān ast"* or "Isfa-han is half of the world." I was anxious to see if the proverb was true, so I took the one-hour flight south to Isfahan where I began my language immersion experience with the Khorasani family who had accepted me as a student. My father paid them well for their trouble. By the time of my arrival I knew the basics of conversational Farsi, so I was able to converse with the parents and their children, Afsin and Afsoon. The wife, Leila, said, "You're most welcome in our home. For your time here, you are like one of my children." Even so, she covered her hair whenever I entered the kitchen for meals.

I had a small room to myself where I could study late into the night. The children were in bed by nine. During the day I was permitted to attend classes at the University of Isfahan, again thanks to the arrangements of my father. I sat in on two religious classes,

Islamic Jurisprudence and Ijtihad, or Islamic Reasoning in Sharia Law. The professor of jurisprudence began the class, "I do not allow questions during class. I teach only the truth. You do not need to know anything else." The all-male attendees spoke only to each other, making minimal eye contact with me. Was I an intruder into their world of complex Islamic thought? Although I grasped the words, I understood little of the religious reasoning that was taught, and I cared less. No exams for me in this discipline.

I completed four months there in my junior year and another four at the first part of my senior year. The father, Khalid Khorasani said, "You speak Farsi like a native."

My visit with the Khorasani family became complicated when Afsin, their twelve-year old son, came to me about a recurring dream. "I get this dream all the time, and I don't know what it means. I see myself trying to get out of a mud hole. I can't breathe. I'm suffocating. The mud hole is in the courtyard of the Sheikh Lotfollah mosque. You know how important the mosque is to our people. I'm surrounded in the hole by pigs squealing. They're trying to escape the mud hole too. The pigs are trying to bite me and eat me."

He was right about that possibility. Pigs were omnivores, and he couldn't tell his parents about this. They would see the dream as a condemnation of the revered mosque and perhaps Islam itself, and so he had come to me. "I saw myself in the dream, swearing insults against God." Afsin considered himself a good Muslim so this frightened him. However, the important part of the dream was his rescue. "Then a white robed man came down from the sky and pulled me out of the mud. He washed me with clear water and placed me on a rock beside the mud hole."

Afsin asked me what I thought of the dream and the fact that it continued to occur regularly. I explained to him he had seen a picture of his rescue by God's grace, and that the white figure was Jesus Himself. But I delivered too much information too soon. I should have allowed him to figure it out on his own. Afsin responded, his eyes wide with fear. "What will I tell my parents? They'll kill me. I don't want to be rescued by Jesus."

"Jesus has already done it. You mustn't tell your parents. It's too soon. There may be a right time," I reassured him. "You'll know if the time ever arrives." As I considered what happened to Afsin, the psalms of my childhood invaded my heart. "O Lord, you have searched me and known me! You know when I sit down and when I rise up:; you discern my thoughts from afar" (Psalm 139:1-2). I could see how this psalm applied to Afsin, but did it apply to me?

I had never before interpreted a dream, other than my own to myself, but this would not be the last time. The meaning of the dream and its repetition were all too clear. Iran, as I was to discover, was a tempestuous sea of dreams — dreams that would entangle me, just as they had ensnared Joseph, my biblical namesake.

Meanwhile, the controversy over Iranian nuclear power continued in the news. Western governments, with the U.S. in the lead, continued stopgap measures to ramp up economic sanctions against Iran. Iran began enriching uranium at its underground Fordow plant, and the Western sanctions against Iran had no effect on their nuclear progress. Iran had already begun loading fuel into the Bushehr power plant. The Persians were too smart: This should have been clear to the West. United Nations' inspectors found uranium at the Fordow plant enriched to twenty-seven percent, a level greater than required for energy production but still far from that essential for a nuclear weapon. In the middle of this ongoing nuclear controversy, the international sanctions had a significant effect on Iran's economy with the rial losing eighty percent of its value. Tehran currency traders rioted.

When the semester ended, it was time to leave the Khorasani family. The mother and father both cried as we parted. They had accepted me as a surrogate son, and had treated me as one of their own. Leila said, "You must promise to return as soon as you can." My most difficult parting was with Afsin. In helping him convert, I had betrayed the family's trust. We had a secret we couldn't share – not with anyone.

By the time I left, Afsin was silently a strong brother in Christ. I had been able to obtain a Farsi translation of the New Testament for him. "You must keep it hidden from your parents," I told him. I felt guilty about the deception, but we had no choice; to do otherwise would have been dangerous for Afsin, me, and for his family.

In my last semester at King's College I dived into my courses and completed the required senior thesis. I chose the economic markets that remained open to Iran during the Western sanctions as my topic. My time in Isfahan had allowed association with Dr. Davoud Al Madani, an economics professor at the university. We met many times at one of the many coffeehouses around the school. "Yusef," he had counseled me, "this is what we must do. You use your family influence to return to Iran, and I will set up the necessary contacts here in Isfahan with companies in those countries not controlled by the sanctions. The U.S. has totally ignored Asia, Africa, and the little countries of the Far East. They always have, and now these countries have developed ways of getting around their sanctions. The U.S has actually issued thousands of exceptions for those with close relationships with your president. And with your talents, we can make a fortune." There were, indeed, considerable opportunities in the unaffected markets. I saw this phenomenon as an opening for myself. My plan for the future remained intact.

I graduated with honors and received the Holbart Prize for the most innovative senior thesis. The reviewers were not pro-American.

By then I was reading the *Tehran Times* regularly online. A small post mentioned the name Esau Allison, a so-called Kuwaiti investor, named as a principal in an arms deal with Yemen. How odd. Why was he involved with Persian business dealings? Wasn't little Kuwait enough for him? Surely he wouldn't be on my doorstep here. But if he turned up, I was going to be ready.

I returned to Kuwait in the summer of 2013 after my graduation. After passing through the passport check station for Kuwaiti citizens, which was always quick for men, I picked up my luggage and proceeded through the baggage inspection area without being stopped. Meanwhile, a Kuwaiti woman with three small children and ten bags was halted, all ten bags opened and their contents, underwear and all, were strewn on the inspection table. *So much for Hibah's "women's rights,"* I mused.

My father met me in the high-ceilinged greeting area, and the bright lights and huge crowd overwhelmed me for a moment. Oddly, my legs buckled. I recovered promptly before my father saw me. We went out into the choking heat, he in his white dishdasha and me in my blue polo shirt and cream slacks. The weather change between London and Kuwait was always shocking, but the Mercedes AC managed the heat.

I had come at the request of my father who was 75. When I saw he was more relaxed than I had ever seen him, I was comforted. He smiled at me, and I thanked the Lord. He had finally recovered from the social rejection he had experienced as a consequence of his fleeing Kuwait during the first Iraq war in 1990. He was reintegrated in the community, and our family reputation was intact again. Binyamin, now ten years old had accompanied him, and he squeezed me around the waist, burying his face in my trousers, laughing all the while.

We proceeded down the Magwa Road to Ahmadi. "Yusef, you won't believe the progress of the Christian movement among Kuwaitis. It's surpassed anything I'd hoped for. My greatest sadness is the death of Dhuwahi last year. He finally couldn't breathe anymore. And for some reason, I've been made leader of the group. Hibah says otherwise, but I think it's only because I'm old."

Surely the numbers had not increased all that much. They still operated *sub rosa.* "Papa, how many Arab believers are there now?" The traffic slowed and formed a line as five camels crossed the road from left to right.

"We meet in more than twenty-five homes in cells of six men. The cells choose different days of the week to meet to avoid an obvious pattern. My old friend John Friedecker advises the whole group. He's been in Kuwait for so many years no one suspects his involvement in anything organized. He also distances himself from the details for his safety and ours."

Four more camels waited their turn on the left side of the road and then proceeded as one driver honked and waved. The little boy herding the camels whacked the last one on the rump and the parade was over. *If camels still crossed major highways, how could anything else in Kuwait change very fast?* The mix of past and present persisted.

"John has given us several rules, which he says are working in other Arab countries. We continue to attend Friday mosque. It's not the long-term plan, but it's safest for this time. We can't meet together for active worship. No new members can be brought in without the recommendation of two current members, and they can't inform their extended families. And finally, multiple wives are discouraged unless they're already present prior to entry into the group."

I asked, "What about the women? What are they told?"

"We leave this up to each man. It is, however, encouraged that all male believers try to bring their wives to Jesus and then work through the Scriptures with them." My father continued his description as he gestured with both hands, still driving. I was apprehensive about our safety. "The number of Kuwaiti believers is about 150 men. We're thankful that so far there is no mention of us in the news, and the Kuwaiti secret police are either uninformed or uninterested. They have more serious threats. There are terrorist elements in the community who see it as their mission to overthrow the monarchy." My father had lost his fear of the secret police. "My real concern is still Esau. He's onto us and our plans."

"What's the next step? What will happen as the number of men grows? When do you think their existence will become known?" I was more worried than my father.

"The Lord knows the answer to those questions. It's not one of the burdens I carry. I think it'll be years that we must remain in secret – unless something happens to change the whole makeup of the society. I'm tired. I've been through more than I want to remember. I'm content with today." I saw he really was satisfied.

We pulled into the driveway of our home and my father pressed the automatic gate opener on the visor. Binyamin hopped out first and ran to Hibah. I got out of the car and slipped on the day's accumulation of dust on the driveway. What a contrast between the green of England and the dust of Kuwait.

Since I was not one of the regular, approved men in the group of Kuwaiti believers, I was not invited to any of the sessions, even those in our own home. I was told to remain in my room. It hurt me that my half-brother Thawab was there regularly for the meetings, but I understood the risks of any other course of action. In regular attendance was a son of my martyred Uncle Suhayb. I had never known my father's brother. The Iraqis had killed him during the invasion while I was still an infant. He was a hero of the Kuwaiti resistance.

For my brief time at home I faced the awkwardness of my current relationship with Hibah. She still blamed me for leaving, and her greeting revealed that. She extended her hand, but there did not embrace me. We only talked during meals. "We missed you here in Kuwait," she said quietly one evening. "Our father is OK, but he still regrets your leaving. He's needed you, Yusef; not that it matters at all to you. You always do what's best for yourself instead." Her voice was low, but pain and accusation filled her eyes.

Her words lay on the table between us like a loaded gun. I thought it best to limit my response, so I changed the subject.

"How is your law practice going?" I asked lightly. She didn't reply.

Hibah was now a young woman, still in our home since a Christian Kuwaiti had not been located for her as a husband. Our mother had raised her well, and Hibah was content to wait for the Lord's timing. Or at least she didn't speak of it.

Binyamin was already a computer whiz kid, engaged in special summer computer classes at Kuwait University. He already knew how to code, and while I was there, attempted to give me a little lesson, which I failed.

For the moment, Esau, still at the Al Ahli Bank, was quiet, perhaps waiting for the next opportunity. There were rumors he had all kinds of extremist ties, from the Saudi Wahhabis to al-Qaeda to ISIL (which is also known as ISIS in America especially). Since the first mention of the Wahhabis so long ago, I had learned they were regarded by many in the world as one of the strictest, most orthodox Islamic groups in the world, centered in Saudi Arabia, although some disagreed with that assessment. Al-Qaeda was well-known for their attacks on the American World Trade Towers and Pentagon in 2001. ISIL was yet another extremist group that believed it was their destiny to rule a strict Islamic regime over the entire Middle East from Turkey to Palestine, even stretching into northern Africa. Although each of these groups were different in their goals, Esau was definitely in cahoots with the most extreme elements of Sunni Islam. And then there had been the note in the *Tehran Times*. He had just married for the third time, keeping two of the three wives. On one occasion, he had been observed visiting the Emir's palace in Kuwait.

I planned to return to Kuwait only rarely. I did not think important events would occur in stodgy Kuwait until most of the other Gulf countries had passed through the fire. That same year, 2013, the reformist-backed cleric Hassan Rouhani won the presidential election in Iran. I took his election personally, believing it was a favorable event for my plans. In September he told an American broadcaster that Iran would "never" build nuclear weapons. He allowed the opening of more coffeehouses as a token of the freedom of the youth. More than half the Iranian population was under thirty. In November, Iran agreed to curb uranium enrichment and gave foreign inspectors better access. Temporarily, the situation cooled.

While I remained in Kuwait, Professor Al-Madani continued to deal with Iranian trading arrangements through countries not participating in the sanctions. The financial opportunities carved out by the sanctions were immense, and both Al-Madani and I intended to take advantage of them. "Young man, the risks for you are great, but so is the reward. Your talents and language skills are beautifully suited to this situation that our present politics has created."

It was to my advantage that the sanctions continued. There seemed to be little doubt they would as the U.S. would not back off; and despite Rouhani's denials, Iran was single-minded in its goal to achieve nuclear independence. I assured Al-Madani I wanted to return to Isfahan because of my contacts there with him, and he located an Iranian trading firm with an office in the city. Much sooner than I expected, I was ready to return and join the Persia Trading Company in Isfahan. *What would Al-Madani expect from me?*

CHAPTER 6

ISFAHAN

In mid-September I arrived at Isfahan Shahid Behesti International Airport, which could be mistaken for any modern airport with its big signs, escalators, plastic seats and stone pillars. Having learned earlier that the orange cab company was the most reliable, I took one into the city. The driver submitted to my price after he realized it was not my first trip, and I was careful to say *darbast*, meaning I wanted to be the only passenger.

Out of respect for the Khorasani family and a desire to maintain contact with Afsin, I went to their home in the Mehrabad section of the city near the Zayandehof River. The father said, "Afsin, why don't you give Yusef a hug." Afsin looked down and obeyed his father, but did not linger on my shoulders. *Was he afraid? Perhaps he no longer believed.* After a night in my old room, like a child returning home, the oddity of the visit assaulted me. I was not their child, and I had betrayed the family's trust by playing a role in Afsin's conversion. I did not belong here. The best thing I could do for Afsin, whether he still believed in Jesus or not, was distance myself from him. Being connected to me would never help him. Perhaps the little boy saw the same facts stretching before us.

In the cab from their apartment to my own, giddiness swept over me, a sensation of escape. I settled into my comfortable, second floor walk-up on Ferdosi Street near the bridge, where I could see the river if I stood on wooden chair at the window.

My salary was generous by Iranian standards: sixty million rials a month. I quickly walked to the nearest store and bought a nineteen-inch Samsung TV to assist with my Farsi, keep up with Iranian news, and, of course, the soccer scores.

Game results were interrupted by the news from *Al-Jazeera*. There she was, sitting at the news desk with her male colleague. The billing on the TV read "Tahara Al-Thani" alongside the name of her cohost, a name forever forgotten. How could a simple TV appearance stun me so deeply? Was it her directness, as if she was flirting at me through the camera? No, it wasn't that. She was just breathtakingly beautiful with a forthright clarity of expression I found irresistible. And her name, Al-Thani: Was she related to the Qatari royal family? Probably not. Could I be smitten from TV appearance?

My first dinner in the apartment was takeout from the Fardis restaurant on the street below me. I chose *beryooni* and watched the cook mince the baked mutton and lungs and then heat the mix over an open fire as he dusted cinnamon on top. But it was not as tasty as that made by my surrogate Persian mother, Mrs. Khorasani. The Persian fast food restaurant, Boof, would be my next stop, for sure.

###

Two days later I reported for work at the Persia Trading Company where I met my boss, Sami Hosseini, an obsequious, paunchy, twitchy man in his fifties. Even as boss, I guessed he was fearful of losing his job. "You must take care here. Anyone may be listening." *Who were these nameless ears?* I was Kuwaiti and therefore unafraid.

He took me by the hand down the hall. "This will be your office. I trust you'll find it satisfactory." *He was my supervisor. Why would he care whether it was satisfactory?* The office had a view of the river. The other employees who had been there for longer periods looked on, glowering, lips parted, several cracking their knuckles. *Were there any among them resentful enough of my position to be dangerous? Was it in this group I would find the "listeners" he warned about? And why was he warning me in the first place? Why was he afraid?* To them, he said, "Gentlemen, please come and welcome Mr. Al-Tamimi." Still, they shook my hand firmly, and after they heard I was fluent in Farsi, several spoke words of greeting. Because of my status as a rich Kuwaiti, some were even animated in their gestures. Perhaps to court my favor?

###

Iran's foreign trade had been battered by sanctions, particularly after the European Union had joined the restrictions. But there were considerable alternatives for financial gain. In June 2012 the U.S. had exempted India, South Korea, Malaysia, South Africa, Sri Lanka, Taiwan, and Turkey from economic sanctions if they cut their imports of Iranian oil. There remained many other trade areas that could be plumbed by the wise, as well as many other countries that had no intention of pleasing America and the other Western nations.

In my first week, a prominent Chinese trading group brought a translator who spoke English, and the advantage fell to me. Our Chinese guests came nodding and smiling to the office, and it was a spectacle. Their bowing and plastic smiles were almost more than I could take, but the negotiations were fruitful and Hosseini broadcast the results to the office staff, "Yusef has brought our Chinese friends into the fold." I was embarrassed, but Hosseini beamed over my achievement, and his tics vanished for the moment. The employees in cubicles in the office center grinned whenever I passed.

Western sanctions had damaged the firm's revenue, as was evident by their old computers in need of replacement and the rasping swivel chairs. The deal I struck went a long way toward alleviating that loss. Hosseini put in an order for new equipment the afternoon of my triumph. The status afforded me because of this contract was one to which I had been accustomed all my life, and its occurrence now lured me into a false sense of security. I arranged for my university contact, Al-Madani, to get a cut as a consultant. No problem for Hosseini: such extraordinary, even unethical, arrangements were commonplace.

But somehow Esau invaded. On a deal I was about to conclude, his name appeared among the signatories. The commission we were promised was suddenly halved, and Hosseini was forced to back out of the arrangement. "Yusef, how did you mess this up?" I shrugged my shoulders, but I knew. On a video business call I saw Esau in the background. His sardonic smile was unmistakable, and he had gained some weight. *How did he have connections so far afield from Kuwait?*

###

I established a regular Thursday presence at a coffee shop on Felestin Street, where I soon made friends with several young men. Multiple (but ancient) TV sets blasted out national soccer games, often Persepolis versus Esteghial (meaning independence) at the shop. These were our initial excuse for sitting together. The 100,000 attendees at the local games made their cheers heard for miles around the stadium. No women were allowed at the games – too many men in shorts, thus providing intolerable stimulation for the ladies.

The coffee shop's iron tables on the concrete sidewalks rattled with the passing autos, and the car exhaust choked us. The traffic never ceased. My friends pointed out the *Gasht-e Ershad* (Guidance Patrol) vans that roamed the larger squares. Through the vigilance of the occupants of these vehicles, the morals and propriety of our apparel was assured.

Weeks passed before the conversations deepened. The four I was close to described themselves as Muslim, but seemed secular in their worldview. They did not stop for prayer time, sported Nike tennis shoes, wore knockoff American-style blue jeans, and read magazines that extolled American movies, most of which were not legally shown in Iran. As in most of the Gulf States, they bought whatever movies they wanted from video pirates.

Two, Abbas and Shaheen, often kept me up late into the evening with their discussions. They couched their thoughts as philosophical but really they were religious in nature. "Can we really believe in anything?" they often asked. It seemed they were in a contest, each to outlast the other so that one would tire and depart, leaving the other with me alone.

Shaheen won first. After Abbas left at 10:30 one night, Shaheen pulled his chair nearer to mine and ordered us both another Turkish coffee. The drink was thick, strong, and definitely eye-opening. He lowered his voice, pulled even closer, indicating that he did not want our conversation overheard. The fact that he was the son of a local cleric indicated to me his thoughts were in the realm of the religious and that he deemed secrecy necessary.

"Yusef, we're friends now, and I want us to keep confidences as friends do. I'm really troubled. I know I'm responsible to my father, but I have thoughts I can't discuss with him. I sense from what you've said during our evenings together that you're more broad-minded. Perhaps you can tell me what's happening to me. I'm having disturbing, recurrent dreams. I don't know what to do about them."

Dreams again. I dreaded what might be waiting for me behind the dream door. "Everyone has dreams," I replied nonchalantly. "They probably are not of any importance."

"I know that, but my dreams have become strange to me." He fidgeted with his prayer beads. *Had the ninety-nine names of God failed him?* "I don't know what the dreams mean. All I know is that they are stressful. I wake sweated and afraid. I'm frightened, really frightened about what they mean." He held his hands near his mouth, perhaps to conceal his words from lip readers. *How risky was this?* People in Iran were frightened of those who watched.

I avoided where this might be leading. "Most of the time, I think, dreams don't really mean anything at all. They just take a common form, like fleeing from danger with no available refuge. Sometimes they're a sexual fantasy, perhaps for release. Or they may stem from things we are worried about or jobs we must do that are not done, like a school assignment. When we wake, we find there was no such task. Don't be troubled by these patterns." I tried to minimize the importance of the dream before he told me about it. I moved my chair back from his, instinctively trying to avoid the coming trouble.

"No, I know the dreams you're talking about, and that kind does not bother me. As you say, everyone has those. These are different and there are two of them: two different, but related, dreams. In the first I find myself riding on a black horse in the middle of a road surrounded by poor women and children on each side. They're hungry and crying. I have two bags filled with food. I'm not even hungry, but I don't give them any of my food. The road

81

is long and seems to have no end, but still I ride on and fail to act."

I replied, "What do you think the dream means?"

"I don't know, but it makes me feel really guilty. I have never ridden a black horse down such a road, but my family is rich and we don't share what we have."

"That is true of so many of us. And the second dream?"

"That dream frightens me even more. In the second dream I'm riding the same black horse down the same road and the starving people are still there. But coming toward me, riding on a white horse, is a man in a bright, white robe with terrible scars on his hands. The man puts his hand on my shoulder and tells me he forgives me. I ask how anyone can forgive me. He doesn't answer but I feel the power of his forgiveness, and for a time I feel free of what I've done. I turn my horse around and distribute my bags of food to the people. And then I awaken, and soon the guilt I felt returns. Both dreams keep repeating, one after the other."

"Who is the man in white?" I questioned. I kept a straight face, avoiding any hints.

"I'm afraid to say what I think. I'm afraid what my father would say," he blinked rapidly.

"Then you know who it is. What are you going to do?"

"That's what I'm asking you."

"I've seen this before. Your course is already mapped out for you, but I can't tell what to do. This is your decision."

Shaheen continued, "The trouble is that I don't know anything about Jesus. There, I've said it. I've said His name. I haven't told anyone else."

"Well, I can get a Bible for you. Then you can read for yourself about who Jesus is. Don't tell your father though." I left him alone, sitting with his unfinished coffee. The rust from the iron tables stained the sidewalk.

So, it began. A week later Abbas went through the same exercise, not the same dream, but one with the same theme. It occurred to me that he and Shaheen had communicated because of the similar course of the conversation, but Abbas denied telling anyone else. Still, the comparisons were striking. I knew the cost of these discussions could be high, and truth be known, I was more concerned with that price than their value. What would the cost be to me? *Why had I engaged in this religious intrigue in the first place?* I was not some sort of strong Christian by any means. I should not be taking these risks, but I could not resist showing off my skills, and somewhere deep within me, I knew I should help these men find the real God.

In January 2014 following talks in Geneva, Iran, the U.S. and Great Britain began implementing a program to deal with Iran's nuclear facilities. In April the International Atomic Energy Agency said Iran had neutralized half its enriched nuclear stockpile.

The tension between America and Iran remained high, and there were large, periodic demonstrations reported in the streets of Tehran and Isfahan featuring the chant, "Death to America." I asked Abbas why they were saying that. "We like Americans," he explained, "It's just the American government. If you look closely, you will see men in suits passing out flyers to the crowd. The crowd is instructed what to do." As I looked, I saw that there were more than a few of these unsmiling men in dark suits mingled in with the people.

Such was the context into which the dream conversions entered. I knew it was not proper to call them conversions, as they were not yet corroborated. From all I'd heard about similar occurrences in Iran, I suspected these were not the last. These could lead me to dangerous ground in the political and social morass in Iran.

Even so, I gloried in Iran's complex and beautiful society. After all, God had foreordained what was happening with these men, and all that would happen thereafter. My mother's psalms invaded my consciousness, and her memory forced me to see His hand: "The heavens declare the glory of God, and the sky above proclaims his handiwork … In them he has set a tent for the sun" (Psalm 19:1,4b). Whatever the strength of my own faith, I couldn't deny what I saw.

Even with the distractions of the dreams, I continued to be the star employee of the Persia Trading Company. I continued in a position of praise, one to which I had grown accustomed as my father's favorite growing up. All this attention confirmed my youthful dreams and plans.

Abbas and Shaheen had dispatched my other Thursday evening coffee partners and monopolized me. I supplied both with Bibles, and our café discussions became quite open. One evening we focused on the story of the Pharisee and the tax collector. Their prior ideas of religion placed the Pharisee at the higher position of the two. After all, he knew the most about religion.

"The Pharisee is a good citizen. He's the one to be praised," argued Abbas. The correct actions and superior knowledge of the Pharisee were, to Abbas, deserving of tribute. They were troubled that God turned away from the Pharisee.

When I explained the underhanded role of tax collectors in the society of that day, they were even more upset. "Why would God turn to the one who had done wrong, the one who stole from others?"

I let them figure this out based on their own experiences. "Why did God seek you out? Did you deserve it?" The tax collector at least acknowledged his wrongdoing on his own. Only now did Abbas and Shaheen do so. "So in your situations, Abbas and Shaheen, God sought you out first. Are you the Pharisee or the tax collector of the story?"

Not long after this, Ferouz joined us. He had contacted Abbas after a brief meeting at a mosque, and accompanied Abbas and Shaheen to our evening sessions. Why had Ferouz made the connection? It didn't compute. Ferouz was longhaired, disheveled, and perhaps a seeker of sorts, but had not had any dreams. He was more in the category of a disaffected youth who had parental conflicts and a record of minor misbehaviors, including drug offenses. He had been arrested for participating in illegal demonstrations against the Ayatollah, from which his father had extracted him. His parents had gone to great lengths to disengage him from his drug-dealing comrades and other brushes with the authorities. They had the means to do so. I wasn't certain if he was sincere or simply rebellious. Had I known his father's position in the beginning, I would have cut off all dealings with Ferouz right away. His father was a member of the Ministry of Intelligence and Security. All their ministers must have a degree in *ijtihad,* or the certified ability to interpret the Quran and the sayings of the Prophet. His father would not be an easy dodge.

Our meetings continued regularly until Abbas called me one morning while I was at work. "Yusef, we could be in trouble." His voice quavered. He wouldn't reveal what was wrong over the phone, but urgently asked that we meet at noon. We met on Masjad-Sayyed Street where we each bought a lamb *shawarma* with the meat shaved off the circular slab rotating in front of the gas burner. The meat was placed on flatbread along with sliced lettuce, tomatoes, and yogurt. We sat together on a bench. Abbas didn't eat; the shawarma remained untouched.

Abbas said, "I'm afraid we've made a big mistake bringing Ferouz into our discussions."

"How's that? I know he's immature, but perhaps it'll come to something."

"Yusef, I think it's all an act. I think his father put him up to it. We both know the status of his father."

I put my lunch aside. "Then we're finished, and I'm Kuwaiti. Who knows what they'll do to me?" I thought of the hiking Americans who had been arrested. But after a moment, I recovered. "But maybe there's a way out. I have an idea." My first thought was for my own safety. *Why was that always my fallback position?*

"I think we should escape. We'll make a run for it, maybe to the north to Baku." said Abbas.

"To where? We can't just leave. We've nowhere to go. What would we do in Baku? And we have no visas for Azerbaijan. No, let's go with my idea." My talent for treachery surfaced. "The three of us, you, Shaheen, and I will go to Ferouz's father and report *his* activities. After all, he told us he wanted to leave Islam. His father will thank us, say he is going to discipline Ferouz, and that will be the end of it. We'll be done with him."

As the eldest of our group, I phoned Hamad Amirzadeh, Ferouz's father, and asked permission for the three of us to visit him. I asked him not to include his son, and we met in his office the next day. The office was all wood panel and imitation gold trim. The thick-bearded Amirzadeh was stiff and unsmiling, no tie, collar open, as was the custom for higher government officials. He sat behind his massive desk, ramrod straight with a computer to his left, and a large Quran between himself and us. The Quran was so large that he couldn't possibly ever hold it and read from it.

As I glanced to my right on his computer screen, I got a glimpse of an e-mail – from Esau Allison! Surely, I was wrong. Why would Esau with ISIL contacts be in communication with Amirzadeh, a strict Shia of the cleric class? It made no sense. When he saw the direction of my gaze, he clicked off the page.

I addressed him first. "Peace be unto you, Hamad Amirzadeh. We bring news to you that we would rather not have to share, but given your honored position, and the still existent possibility of setting your son on the right path, we've come. Your son has been meeting with us for several weeks. We're afraid he wants to leave Islam."

Amirzadeh showed no emotion and didn't respond, never altering his posture.

Abbas filled the silence. "He's a good boy, but he's immature. Perhaps we led him on by listening. We didn't intend to do this, and we won't meet with him again."

"We trust you'll be patient with him. He's just a young man searching for his way. He knows nothing else but Islam."

Amirzadeh still showed no expression. He rose, thanked us for coming, and nodded at the door, indicating we should leave. He never said good-bye in the traditional way. We uttered the standard phrase of departure, "*khoda hefez*" (or "May God be your guardian"), and left quickly. I closed with my right hand briefly on the left side of my chest, a traditional indication of respect and affection.

The three of us gathered outside the building for a moment and wondered if we had achieved our goal. Amirzadeh was highly intelligent, and probably understood our motives. If Ferouz had worn a recorder and taped our conversations, we were lost. We had no way of knowing. We agreed to wait two weeks before resuming our meetings, and then make a better plan for our own protection. We saw no more of Ferouz; we had done our best.

When we reconvened at the coffee shop in two weeks, we were all relieved that no other threat had surfaced. We knew the Iranian secret service were patient though, and might be waiting to collect additional evidence. "We mustn't give them any opportunity to trap us," I said. I proposed simple, clear-cut guidelines. The three of us leaned forward, necks taut. "First, there can be no discussion of Christianity with anyone at all. Second, we must avoid leaving out Bibles and other materials that might be found when we're not at home. Any of our haunts might be searched. Third, for a month, we'll not discuss our beliefs with anyone outside our group of three. After that, we'll reassess the risks." The best we could hope for was no news.

I remained confident in the strength of my own position – from a rich Kuwaiti family, an honored guest of the Iranian government, with a job in which I was a remarkable success. They needed me to circumvent the Western sanctions, after all. But most of all, I trusted in my ability to analyze my way through any situation and come out on top. In short, I attributed my fortunes in life to my unusual qualities and skills. All this was accurate, I was certain of it.

I had just concluded another profitable arrangement, this time with an Indonesian investment group, and my confidence was high; my head erect; and my white shirt, well-starched. Thus, it was with little concern that I accepted the approach of Shabaz Tehrani, a coworker at the trading company. He was a quiet man with horn-rimmed glasses and thick lenses from whom I had heard only pleasantries. I should have wondered why he sought me out at this particular time. The words of a psalm came to me but I ignored them: "Save, O Lord, for the godly one is gone; for the faithful have vanished from among the children of man. Everyone utters lies to his neighbor" (Psalm 12:1-2). My mother had prepared me for this time, but I dismissed her counsel, even as the Word of God she had planted within me spoke.

Shabaz opened the conversation in an odd way. "Yusef, you're so successful in everything here. I understand your family is Christian."

What was the connection between success and being a Christian? How did he know I was a Christian? I had not spoken of my family to anyone in the office. I gave no response.

"It's important we're private in our conversations. But I have many questions I want to ask you. I hope you can share your experiences with me."

"Shabaz, why are we having this conversation? What is this about?" I tried to lead him to a private area of the office.

"I understand you're a Christian. I want help with certain questions."

"Then, let me talk to you to see what your understanding is about being a Christian. You can decide for yourself if I am a Christian. I am not saying one way or the other." I was careful not to admit my status; but if he was truly a seeker, I didn't want to reject him. My lack of denial of being a Christian was undoubtedly equal to a full admission. For a moment I felt vulnerable, particularly in view of our recent encounter with the Amirzadeh family, but I allowed the exchange to continue anyway.

I should have opted out of the conversation, but I ignored my own recurring dream. Again the Joseph effect haunted me. In the dream I saw a man shackled and imprisoned with no trial. Confident of my position, I did not allow myself to see the dream's interpretation. Surely my family situation and native skill would shelter me from harm.

"Yusef, I was, of course, reared a Muslim. I avoid wrongdoing according to the Quran. I think surely that must be enough, but I hear certain radio stations who say they are Christian. They say being good is not enough. How can this be?"

"What do you mean by 'good'?" I asked.

"I mean doing the right things, not hurting anyone."

"Is there anything else?"

"That's what I'm asking." I should have seen at this point that he was interrogating me. He clearly had no conviction of his own sin. Allah was not working on his conscience. The conversation proceeded in this vein for thirty minutes, questions about what it meant to be a Christian. Eventually, I called a halt to it. I didn't think I had crossed any lines. Others in the office were watching us from their desks.

All this time the international scene continued to buzz in Iran. In June 2014 President Rouhani offered to assist Iraq in its battle against Sunni elements, further enhancing old Sunni-Shia splits. Iranian Revolutionary guards were providing more training to Iraqi militia than the Americans were. Negotiations over Iran's nuclear program were reactivated.

One day, I received an ill-timed and frightening e-mail: "You fell into the trap – you talked with Shabaz. Esau" What did Esau have to do with any of this? Why would he even care about Iran and issues of religion on this side of the Gulf?

When Abbas, Shaheen, and I began to meet again, Abbas told us he thought he was being followed. He had always been the more fearful and suspicious one of the group, so Shaheen and I didn't give this much credence. But when, without a word, he failed to attend the coffee shop the next week, our apprehensions grew. He was quite dependable and his absence was out of character. We called his cell phone multiple times and got no answer. Then, it occurred to us that our own cell numbers might be betraying us, so we ceased calling and waited.

There was no further word for two weeks. Shaheen and I continued to meet for coffee. Then, Shaheen disappeared too. I had no choice, but to go to his home. "I'm a friend of Shaheen. I haven't been able to contact him. I'm worried about him."

His parents, conservative Muslims, had not heard from him for three days. They didn't invite me in. "We've reported his absence to the police. We can't get them to do anything. Dealing with them is even worse than usual." They wanted to know my connection to Shaheen. I simply told them he was my friend from the coffee shop.

I returned to work, trying to remain calm. My boss called me into his office. "Yusef, two men in black suits came to the office looking for you. Whatever you're into, don't involve me." Typical Hosseini.

Did Esau have anything to do with this? How could I have been discovered? Was it via the computer again? Should I never e-mail my friends?

I remained as composed as I could, trying to relax with my hands in my pants pockets. I told Hosseini I had a family emergency in

Kuwait and would need to be gone for about a week. A family emergency always takes precedence in the Middle East. After a fast cab trip to the Behesti International Airport, no luggage, I booked the first available flight out of Iran to Dubai, and then on via Kuwait Airways to Kuwait City. The clerk didn't smile with my booking. "No luggage, sir?" I nodded.

Upon my arrival in Kuwait, my father was sharp with me, no preliminary greeting. "Running away will do no good. They can't touch you. You're Kuwaiti. Just face what's in front of you. You led those two men to Jesus, and you're responsible for them. There's just no way they'll challenge a Kuwaiti citizen. You're safe by virtue of your birth and position." My father's confidence buoyed me up. Surely he was right.

Was there any other choice but to return and help Sheehan and Abbas? I feared my father underestimated the risks, but he was my father.

The growth of the gospel in Kuwait during my brief absence had been exponential, but was still secret. Perhaps that's what made my father so strong. "God will not be mocked," he assured me. "The gospel will grow and bear fruit, no matter what. Yusef, what do you really believe? You must know the Lord will protect you." Thus, he stirred up my old uncertainties. I was not as clear on that matter as I had hoped, and I began to wonder. I depended on my charm and abilities, but it was becoming obvious that they might be insufficient. So how was my father so confident? He was clearly trusting God in a way that I did not.

Hibah joined the conversation and did not encourage me as she had done in the past. "Yusef, Allah has given you all you wanted in Iran. You wanted to be there, and He clearly has work for you there."

In the end, it was with fear and reluctance that I returned to Isfahan. *What am I doing?* On arrival I was taken aside at the immigration desk for non-Iranians and escorted into the office of a very polite official dressed in an expensive, gray, pin-striped suit. There was a single manila folder on his desk. "I'm very sorry for delaying you," he said with a smile. I noted he didn't use the word "detain." The staff brought us tea, and he left his desk chair and joined me, sitting at the table. He put his hand on my shoulder briefly, as if to say *we are brothers.*

"There are some routine matters that need clarification. I see in the reports you have made many close friends during your time in Isfahan." He patted the folder on the table in front of us.

"Yes, certainly, I'm very happy here in your country." I tried to remain unperturbed, but sweat was gathering in my armpits.

"I see you had two close friends, Abbas and Shaheen. I'm afraid we've had to collect them and interrogate them. Initially, they didn't have much to say; but in the end, they were quite forthcoming." *Why was he speaking of them in past tense? What did he mean by "in the end"?* "We know they were apostates. They left Islam. They said you helped them. Mr. Al-Tamimi, you're from a Kuwaiti family, a clan bent on trouble for your little country. We have information about all of you from your half-brother." *Esau*

95

again? How had he come into the picture? My stomach contracted. "It would be much easier for you and our two countries if you simply got back on the plane and returned to Kuwait. We would prefer that. I'm afraid this is a pivotal moment for you."

I fell silent for a full minute. I thought back to my father's assurances of safety and also to Hibah's dare. Looking back, I'm sure my family had no idea what Iran was really like. My self-image directed me to show courage even when there was none. "Sir, I've done nothing wrong. I have a good job here in Isfahan, and I love it here. I would like to remain in your great country." Had it not been for my father and Hibah and knowing I would have to face them in Kuwait, I might have purchased an outbound ticket. I was fearful of the Persian authorities, but more anxious about preserving my image and the honor of my family. I should have reversed the order of concern, but pride eclipsed reason.

"So it shall be." With that comment, he pressed a button on the underside of the table. Two thick-shouldered men with full black beards entered the office and each grasped one of my arms. *Where do these guys get those shoulders?* I was taken to an unmarked black Mercedes and driven off into the evening. They did not answer my requests for information, even as my voice shook. The psalms called out to me, "O Lord, how many are my foes! Many are rising against me; many are saying of my soul, 'There is no salvation for him in God'" (Psalm 3:1-2).

After an hour driving northward from the city, we arrived at a large installation that I recognized as Kashan prison. I had heard of it and seen photos, usually depicting executions by hanging.

I was taken to a white-painted room with no windows and one door. One of the men told me to disrobe and provided a loose-fitting white shirt and white trousers. My wallet, apartment, car keys, and cell phone were taken. I sat waiting alone for nearly two hours. Another man, tall and clean-shaven, finally entered the room and sat across facing me. I couldn't move, paralyzed.

"Mr. Al-Tamimi, I can promise you your stay with us will go much easier for you if you cooperate fully. We know you are a Christian who pretends to be a Muslim. Our contacts in Kuwait confirm our information. We know your father in Kuwait is a Christian, and everything about your family." *How do they know? Esau? Why does he care enough to intervene so far afield?* "We know about your friends, Abbas and Shaheen. They confessed their apostasy and paid the penalty for it. We must know who else you have deceived."

"Have I been charged with any crime? I want to know what my rights are. Is there something you have against me?" I cracked my knuckles, trying to display anger. Ineffective.

"We ask the questions, not you. Today, I ask only one question. Who else have you deceived? We will learn everything from your computer."

I couldn't tell him, not ever, about young Afsin. I held off the story of Ferouz and Shabaz, thinking I could occupy the interrogator's efforts later by recounting information they likely already knew. When I supplied no answers to his repeated questions, I was taken to a cell.

The cell was gleaming white, much cleaner than I expected, an image from one of my dreams. For the first two days, all meals were brought to my cell and I was not allowed to meet with other prisoners. Then, on the third day I was taken for interrogation, this time by a straight-laced, uniformed man with a small moustache and goatee.

I concluded he was a member of the Basij, the paramilitary force subordinate to the Iranian Revolutionary Guard Corps. The Basij was heavily involved in the violent crackdowns and serious human rights abuses that had occurred in Iran since that June 2009 contested presidential election. They were also implicated in attacks on university students, abuse of detainees, and violence against peaceful protesters. I told him about Ferouz and Shabaz, that they had sought me out on their own without any instigation from me, and that I had not attempted to lead them into apostasy. All this was true, but cached in cowardly terms. My presumption was that security forces had planted them, and that appeared to be correct because he showed no interest in their stories. He wanted to know about other contacts, explanations of all my previous actions, and my future plans, if they had not apprehended me.

"My future plans are simply to continue working at my firm," I answered, "Why am I here? What's charges have been brought against me? May I leave and go back to my job?"

"No, you will not be permitted to leave."

"When is my trial?" This was to be my continuing question.

I expected to be beaten into some sort of confession, but there were no beatings, just the interminable day following day, each mostly in my cell. *What was going to happen to me? A trial? Surely they would not hold me without a trial.* They would not treat a Kuwaiti citizen as they had treated Shaheen and Abbas.

CHAPTER 7

MY PRISON COMMUNITY

No word of a trial. No answer to questions about any judicial process.

After two weeks I was allowed out of my cell with other prisoners, like a pet released from my cage into the courtyard of the other pets.

Without my imprisonment at Kashan, I would have never have understood, truly grasped, what was happening in Iran. My days were filled with poets, artists, filmmakers, academics, political dissidents, Christian pastors, drug dealers, murderers, thieves, rapists, and most of all, dreamers. No, I don't mean philosophers but normal individuals who had dreams, not just the standard dreams we all experience, but prophetic dreams, dangerous dreams. The history of modern Iran is replete with reports of gospel conversions through dreams, and in the prison I was honored to hear many. Some recognized the meaning of their recurring dreams and others were looking to have their dreams translated. I'm certain some of these dream stories were planted as an attempt to pull me further into the morass. At this point, what difference could it make? Still I saw malevolent intent in every observation and every event; I thought every circumstance was directed only at me.

101

The dreams did not lead to immediate conversion for most. This is a crucial point. They did, however, raise the awareness of a spiritual yearning that could only be satisfied by news of the gospel in sufficient detail. For some, the course of conversion was rapid; in others, erratic. The need for Bibles was crucial, but this necessity was not easily resolved.

My imprisonment provided a strange freedom I would not have experienced in my comfortable position in the city because everyone knew I had been imprisoned because of my Christian beliefs, so there was no longer any reason to hide my faith. Now it could be tested, a trial I did not want. I prayed Psalm 55:1: "Give ear to my prayer, O God, and hide not yourself from my plea for mercy!" But the Lord allowed no escape.

I considered the possible crimes for which I could be held. The most serious crime was my supposed conversion and apostasy from Islam. Apostasy means the abandonment of a previously held belief. The punishment for apostasy from Islam is death. But I had never been Muslim, having been reared and taught in a Christian home. The second, more likely charge, was proselytizing. At no point was either of these charges specifically made to me, and I continued to be held without charges levelled against me or a trial in my future.

###

During the four hours a day out of my cell I was permitted to speak freely with other prisoners. One of my first serious exchanges took place with Kamal Kashani, formerly a literature professor at the University of Isfahan. He was charged with spreading dissent and disobeying government censorship. This issue had arisen in the context of his teaching certain banned literary works. His specific crime was the assignment to his students of the short story titled, "The Baboon Whose Buffoon Was Dead" by Sadeq Chubak. The story is an allegory about a baboon controlled by an all-powerful master, the buffoon. The buffoon represented the unyielding state, a theocracy. On the death of his master, the buffoon, the baboon is forced to make his own sad choices.

I tried to exchange complaints against the system with Kashani, but he replied with, "I don't want to hear about your experiences as a Christian, a foreigner here in my country. You're nothing to me." Thus, he relegated me to the level of one his accusers. Kashani resented his incarceration, and never laughed or smiled. He fired insults and sarcasm at any target. "My family or students won't come to visit me." Surely, his family and students wouldn't visit him because of possible entanglement in the charges against him. He would end each diatribe with, "I know now there is no God." He remained stiff, inflexible, and bitter in his hardened disbelief. In the past a devout Muslim, his resentment against God was profound, and this brought him great personal suffering. Every week he lost visible weight from his already lanky frame.

But God intervened, and his relationship with me softened. He came to me, eyes wet. "Yusef, my sleep is troubled. I'm having a dream that frightens me. A tall man dressed in gold walks toward me. He looks angry. On each occasion, he says, 'You forsake me in your anger.' Then, he turns away from me."

"Who is the man?"

"That's what frightens me. I'm afraid he's going to punish me."

"Why would he punish you?"

"I'm angry with God."

I replied, "Has the God of the Quran ever spoken to you?"

"No."

"Then perhaps he is not the God of the Quran." I closed the discussion at this point.

We talked again in three days, and his demeanor had changed. The permanent frown was gone from his face.

"I think I know who the man is – I think He's Jesus. If someone had told me this could happen, I would not have believed him. The stories I taught my students didn't prepare me for this."

"And if you're right?"

"Then, it means He comes for me. I have not asked Him to come to me, and I've done nothing that would cause Him to come for me. What do you think? Is this possible?" He sat down on the concrete bench with hands together, almost prayerful. *Repentant? I wasn't sure.*

"I believe you're right. This is what I thought from the beginning, but you had to figure it out for yourself. You're not the first to experience such a dream. You must know that the Lord of the world is working out His will." The wind bent down the grass in the prison yard, but Kashani was beyond looking at his physical surroundings, not the scrubby grass or the high, tan walls or the grim-faced guards.

"I'm a teacher. I've always wanted to know more. And now I don't have any way to learn more about Jesus. I need to read His book." His eyes were wet. *Were those real tears?* I wasn't certain.

"You're right. We can talk and I can teach you more, but you need a Bible. I haven't been able to figure out how to get Bibles into the prison."

Two weeks later Kashani introduced me to a guard he had befriended. The guard was a closet Christian. He told Kashani, "I'll bring in one Bible at a time. I'll not take any more risk for you than that." They were tiny volumes containing both Old and New Testaments with miniscule print, but they were easily concealed. Even with my young eyes I couldn't read the print, so we needed magnifying glasses, which required more smuggling. We paid another guard to bring those. We told him they were for the elderly. Handling such contraband would be an added charge on our lists of wrongdoings if discovered, but I had never been formally charged with anything yet. Even so, I was anxious and troubled about the smuggling, and my stomach turned when I thought of the possible consequences. My ability to sleep, which was already poor, nearly disappeared, and my stomach problems, always the mirror of my distress, grew.

Kashani was a quick student with his new Bible and turned out to be a remarkable teacher and evangelist among the inmates. Dreams continued to present themselves. The recipients were thieves, rapists, and insurrectionists – all manner of men. The gospel flourished, albeit quietly. Strangely, the epidemic remained undiscovered for some time. I couldn't believe we had been given such freedom, and I began to see attacks even where there were none.

Once again the words of a psalm, asking for the Lord's protection, came to my aid: "Deliver me from my enemies, O my God" (Psalm 59:1a). It was as if my mother was by my side, reminding me of my heritage. Sometimes I heeded her, sometimes not.

Almost all the prisoners who considered themselves Muslim were Twelver Shias. I knew a bit about Shia theology from my high school religion course. They believed that twelve divinely inspired imams came after Muhammad and that the last imam, the last Mahdi, still existed in hiding, having disappeared from view in the ninth century. In the last days, they believe, this Mahdi will return to public life and fight one final battle against the armies of the Antichrist. He would triumph and rule justly for a period of years, whereupon Jesus (as a prophet) would finally return in triumph from heaven too. Of the Madhi, the Persians said, "May God hasten his return." I saw striking similarities to these predictions and those of Christian end-times theology. The vital difference was that the Twelvers viewed Jesus as a human prophet, and not divine. Still, there remained in this theology a basis for discussion that provided legitimate and open exchange in this odd environment, a situation created unintentionally by the Iranian theocracy.

Dreams, then, with Jesus as the star, provided the crucible in which the divinity or non-divinity of Jesus could be challenged and discussed. Dreamers told non-dreamers about their experiences. Often the questions were: "Why did Jesus come for me and not Muhammad or the last Mahdi? And why would Jesus come for me at all when I rejected Him? Why does He bother with me?"

But not all the dreams were of Jesus. A number of men came to me with their dreams, perhaps for entertainment as much as anything else. I was indeed engaging with my stories of Jesus in the life of my family. Majid Nafisi's dream, however, was not so innocent or entertaining. Majid was imprisoned for the theft of documents pertaining to the illegal financial dealings of those high in the government. He had been convicted in the Public Court of the first level, which dealt with serious crimes. His sentence was five years at Kashan.

"My dream shows me facing a judge I've not seen previously. A noose of coarse rope hangs from the ceiling of the courtroom. I've had the dream three times."

Although the dream seemed strange to him, he disregarded any possible significance for himself personally because he had already been tried and sentenced.

Our meetings all took place in the open courtyard. The weather was cold and rainy, and I had no coat. I had not slept and was in a surly mood. "The meaning is clear. I think you'll be tried again and hanged." A quick, cruel response on my part. His only defense was a forced laugh as he turned his back on me.

But there is no definite end to judicial action in Iran. One verdict can be overturned or changed by another court, even on matters thought settled. Majid received notice the next day that his case would be tried again in the Court of Cassation, a higher court with the right to take up matters resolved in the lower Public Court. His brown skin turned gray. An additional charge was added to the felony of theft: attempting to damage the reputation of the Council of Guardians. The Guardians are twelve jurists, six appointed by the supreme leader and six by parliament. The Council of Guardians holds considerable power, even the voiding of parliamentary action and the approval or disapproval of presidential candidates.

The trial convened the next week and lasted only two days. Majid was allowed to speak to his attorney once, and then only briefly. He was convicted and sentenced to death by hanging. I saw him as he was taken back to his cell in handcuffs and ankle chains. He looked at me without speaking, but his eyes told the story. He spat in my direction. I was sorry I had made such a blunt prediction, which had served no good purpose.

In two days, on a Monday, the sentence was carried out. We were all brought out of our cells to watch. Kashan prison did not use gallows for hanging but a much more efficient, portable apparatus. The hanging rope was suspended from the end of the arm of a small crane-like tractor. The executioner placed the noose around Majid's neck, and the tractor slowly elevated the arm of the crane until he was suspended off the ground. The weight of his generous girth caused his neck to stretch quite remarkably. Death was not rapid with this method as it was with the usual one in which the drop from a gallows was swift enough to dislocate the upper bones of the neck and damage the brain stem, resulting in immediate death. With gradual elevation by the crane, Majid was slowly strangled by his weight instead. For fully five minutes I saw his face contort and his legs jerk rhythmically. How long it takes a man to die!

Many prisoners were aware of my accurate interpretation of Majid's dream and its outcome, and for several weeks most were reluctant to talk with me. But the effect dissipated, and the varied conversations resumed over time.

Although dreams formed the nexus for the introduction of the gospel in Kashan, its spread occurred mainly in the usual manner – new converts telling others about their experiences. If I had not seen this for myself, I would not have believed it. The gospel's mode of entry demonstrated its grace. None of the dreamers had sought Jesus. All knew they had done nothing to deserve His intervention. Through the tiny Bibles that entered Kashan, the converts learned what God had done through Jesus. Before Kashan I believed God's gift to me was dream interpretation; I thought I had the power to manage His grace. But in truth, I was only an observer. I didn't begin to understand what grace meant until Kashan. My imprisonment was God's gift to me. I say this with great hesitation, and it required a great deal of time for the gift to be digested. Even so, a lump remained in my stomach.

And even more strangely, through the fact that most Kashan

prisoners were Shia Muslims, the groundwork was being set in place for the coming of the last days and the return of Jesus. Now those who had formerly awaited the coming of the man Jesus awaited the return of the divine Jesus instead.

During my imprisonment the international scene continued its complicated intricacies unabated. In August 2014 Iran shot down an Israeli drone hear its Natanz uranium enrichment site. In November, Russia, ostensibly to ease Iranian demands to have their own uranium enrichment, agreed to build up to eight nuclear reactors for Iran. Most saw this agreement as Russia's attempt to assist Iran covertly in their nuclear program. Further discussions failed with Western powers, but all parties agreed to an extension for talks to resolve the matter. That Iran would eventually build its own nuclear device was a foregone conclusion; only the timing was in question. Had the world ever prevented any country desiring a bomb from getting it? What a silly thought.

Meanwhile much of the Muslim world was in turmoil due to the spreading activity of the Islamic State of Iraq and the Levant (ISIL). This Sunni group with its extraordinary, ultra-Wahhabi viewpoint had turned the Muslim world upside down. They justified their actions based on Quranic interpretation, which left many Muslim clerics at a loss. ISIL emphasized the singular oneness of God, a position that could not be disputed by monotheists. From this they concluded that anything which interfered with that principle was punishable by death. Most clerics offered no rebuttal, no explanation. For Iran, with its' predominantly Shia population, the situation was somewhat clearer, at least with respect to the threatening Sunni theology. They could disavow the Sunni position and even offer assistance to Iraq, which gave them an increased foothold in that troubled country.

Every trouble in the world is old. All this trouble had begun with the slaying of Hussein, the Prophet's grandson, in the seventh century. Hussein became a hero to the Shia. For a long time, the old strife between the two sects of Islam remained minor. Shia and Sunni families intermarried and lived together in relative peace, but the conflict was spurred on for centuries and in the current age rested mainly in the arms of Sunni Saudi Arabia and Shia Iran, the two opposing groups.

As I sat in my bleak cell it became clear to me that this long-existing Shia-Sunni conflict could be the root of a coming conflagration as yet unimagined by Muslim scholars of the day, and the result would be God's doing, not theirs. The Lord had planted these seeds of struggle for His own purposes. And now my half-brother Esau had entered the fracas. But whom did he favor — the Sunnis or the Shia? Or did it matter to him?

By December 2014 the gospel had grown sufficiently in Kashan that knowledge of its spread could not be avoided. How did the warden let this happen? Strangely, the prison authorities remained oblivious to the events that were blossoming under their noses.

The next week, I learned the prison warden was under investigation by the state for misuse of funds. Perhaps his vision of prison events had been obscured by his personal troubles. He summoned me to his office, where papers were spread all over the table behind his desk. His sandwich of olives and avocados had fallen to the floor, and he was plunging through the documents, perhaps hoping to discover the critical missing piece.

Any such summons to see the warden was urgent. Rashid Mokri was a thick-browed man with a black, curly beard and moustache. He was shy with a deference and quiet demeanor not expected in a prison warden. There was a thick callus on his forehead that could only be acquired with the most persistent, prayer genuflection. He rose, paced, and bit his lower lip.

"Mr. Al-Tamimi, perhaps you've heard there is some question about our financial management here at Kashan." *Why did he think I'd heard? Probably because everyone in the prison had.* "I'm not sure if there is a problem or not, but I see from your dossier that you're educated in the area of money management. I need your help."

"I would be happy to help, but I would need full access to all the prison's financial records to do that," I began. I realized this opportunity could have boundless possibilities. "I must have some idea of the scope of the problem and where the trouble lies."

"I'm afraid I'm being accused for reasons that are unconnected to the actual finances."

"What reasons?"

"Perhaps we can discuss that matter in the future. They are saying that money intended to purchase prison supplies is being siphoned off for other purposes."

"Couldn't the prison accountant check the figures himself?"

"He's the brother of a powerful cleric. They couldn't find any other job for him. I cannot be sure of him."

Mokri took me down to the accountant's office. He was not there and the secretary informed us he had not come in for work for the past week. The office was in a worse mess than the warden's – piles of computer printouts scattered like a trash heap. Spreadsheets lay in disarray, and the computer keyboard was dusty, seemingly untouched for some time.

"You're to take over this office. It's now your responsibility. I'll leave instructions to give the so-called accountant a desk out in the room with the secretary if he ever shows up again. I can only give you a week. Any longer will be too late for me."

I set about the task, which was not intellectually difficult, merely tedious. I gathered the spreadsheets from the floor and desks, organizing them chronologically, as I plowed through the incoming budget and the expenditures. It was quickly apparent that the prison accountant, one Mr. Nouruzi, was not as slow-witted as Mokri had thought, just messy. His mistake, however, was being absent at a critical juncture, leaving the evidence in plain view. There had been no attempt to obscure his diversion of funds; the spreadsheets told the story. Every other biweekly disbursement to the prison had been sent in total to an offsite account. The dust on the computer keyboard reflected the likelihood that he had brought in his own computer to make the transfers. It was a simple matter to take the spreadsheet numbers of the disbursements in question, plug them into the prison computer, and see where they had gone.

The routing number of the receiving bank was the same for all the transfers. All the money had been deposited in the same account at the Saman Bank in Isfahan. I called the bank, gave the account number, and asked the balance. I wasn't sure if they would release the information by phone, but it was the weekend and late in the day, and the lower level bank functionary likely wanted to finish and go home.

"The balance is 41.8 billion rials (about 1.5 million dollars)."

"There must be some mistake. Could you check the name on the account for me?"

"Hafez Nouruzi," he answered. That was the name of the cleric whose brother was the accountant.

"Thanks very much," I replied, clicking off. Other than the clutter in the office, no effort had been made to conceal the transfers.

In two days I presented a detailed written report to Warden Mokri. He was, of course, infinitely grateful. The next issue was on how to report the fraud. Even telling the tale could be dangerous. Mokri decided to submit the report to the administrator of area prisons rather than to the state officials who had raised the accusation against him. After the submission Mokri heard nothing more for two weeks. The accountant never returned to work nor was there any word from him. Mokri did not try to reach him. I was installed as the accountant for the prison until further notice. After the flow of funds was restored, the amount supplied to the prison turned out to be quite generous, and we were able to support a new prison library.

My job was quite simple and was not full-time. It did require my visiting Mokri regularly, and we shared stories – me, of my prison life, and he, of his recent spiritual experiences. We became close friends, and the reason for the apparent tolerance of the gospel in Kashan became clear.

"Why do you have the callus on your forehead? I thought you had that because you were a strict Muslim."

"I'm from a Muslim family. They don't know I've turned to Jesus. I still pray in the same manner, and the callus cuts off questions. It's a common device in Iran among Muslim converts."

"What's going to happen in Kashan?"

"As for me, I'm going to allow the gospel to continue unfettered. We can't stop it anyway." He leaned back in his desk chair, hands clasped behind his head.

"What's going to happen to me? I've not been charged with any crime nor have any outside officials come to meet with me. I'm sure my family wants to know what's happening."

"You now have computer and Internet access. As long as you recognize the computer may be monitored, you may say whatever you want. You can be sure we're all being electronically scrutinized by a variety of means."

The position as the accountant of Kashan placed me at the top of the inmate hierarchy. As such, even greater numbers of inmates turned to me for counsel in all sorts of areas – financial, family, questions about being a Christian, and, of course, dreams.

My imprisonment there extended to July 2015. By that time, negotiations over Iran's nuclear status had become so complicated that there seemed to be no simple conclusion. The Iranians continued with the technique of first agreeing to a plan and then issuing contrary statements to the news networks – all the usual tricks employed by countries desiring to play the international community. Tensions in the country were high because the economic sanctions were affecting the private lives of average Iranians. The negotiations between the U.S. and European nations continued with no resolution. Rouhani and the Foreign Minister Mohammed Zarif pushed the Iranian religious system to cooperate.

Then, suddenly in mid-July, a breakthrough was announced, and an agreement was reached that seemed to satisfy all participants. It was a victory for Iran, even though the text seemed to prevent their getting a nuclear weapon. For Iran, the bomb was in sight, and everyone knew it. The Obama administration and the U.S. negotiators under John Kerry had done all they could. Kerry had continued to work for a resolution, despite breaking a leg in the middle of the negotiations. The resulting agreement allowed the U.S. some modicum of an honorable peace.

###

In Yemen the Houthis with their Shia leanings battled Sunni forces from the Gulf and Egypt. Victory was elusive for both sides. Shia Iran continued their proxy war in Yemen against the Gulf Sunni states, mainly Saudi Arabia. Iraqi Shias were assisted by Iran in fighting against ISIL. Thus, the war between Sunni and Shia took a fixed form with no apparent way out of the gathering conflict. Still, I could see no role for Esau in this struggle between Muslims. Was he using both sides?

###

And then Kashan was over, suddenly and without warning. As I walked toward his office, Mokri was handcuffed and taken away by the secret police under control of the Basij. He looked at me as if to say *I'm sorry.* I presumed it must have had something to do with his reporting of the fraud. Or maybe the many Christian conversions in the prison had leaked out. Two days later they came for me. "We know what's going in here. We know you're responsible."

"Responsible for what?"

They did not respond. I was placed in yet another black vehicle and driven north on Route 7. I went through the options in my head. None were good. Soon we passed the holy city of Qom, a mockery of the word "holy" to me now. In less than three hours we pulled into the reception area of Evin prison. The entry area was an innocent-looking structure with white, horizontally slated siding, bars over the few windows, and a sign in Farsi and English which read "Evin House of Detention"; but Evin was infamous for its torture of so-called political detainees. This prison was on top of any Iranian's I-don't-want-to-go-there list. I never considered ending up there. My arrival was like a nightmare come true.

CHAPTER 8

EVIN

I was taken to a holding cell and informed my questioning would begin the next morning. The cell contained a single water tap, a hole-in-the-floor toilet with a metal grid plate for squatting, and a bed with a thin mattress, no covers. No food. Cold and hungry, I was unable to sleep, my eyes stuck open all night long. Most of all, I was terrified about what the morning would bring.

My interrogator appeared at seven the next day with a blanket, fried egg and cold coffee for me. He introduced himself as Ali. His skills in questioning surpassed those I had encountered before.

"Why have you been brought to Evin?" he asked, looking away in apparent indifference.

I wrapped myself in the blanket and gobbled down the egg in two bites before I answered. "I don't know why I am here. I've not been charged at any point in my detention."

"Surely, you've done something wrong. I understand you admit to being a Christian, so I suppose you left Islam?"

"No. I've been a Christian since birth. I can't be accused of

119

leaving Islam because I was never a Muslim."

"If you're truly a Christian, then perhaps there's some hope for you. If not, then it would appear you're leading others astray, simply for the purpose of causing dissent. And I understand you're a skillful interpreter of dreams – even dreams that lead to apostasy from Islam."

"I don't see where these questions lead."

"First, this is a conversation, not an interrogation. Second, you need not be concerned about where we're headed. You can supply much useful information. I want to know what you mean when you say you're Christian."

This was the most difficult question he could have asked me. *Why would he start with this theological point?* Now I was forced to be clear. "I mean that I believe Jesus is God Himself and that He sacrificed Himself for me by dying on the cross."

"Why was that needed? It seems a waste of divinity. I doubt you're worth it."

"The sacrifice was necessary because I couldn't conquer my sin or pay the penalty for it." These were the standard statements of belief in Jesus as Savior that I had heard all my life.

"Then what is your right to this sacrifice?"

"I have no right to it."

"Then, how dare you claim it?"

I stammered, unable to give a clear response. *Please end this line of questioning.*

Only later did I get it right in my head: the One who sacrificed Himself is the One who offers His sacrifice to the believer. It was a judicial act and therefore a bestowal of right. Did my failed answer reflect the uncertainty that comes to all believers at times, my lack of precision, or was my faith more superficial than I realized? The timing was bad, very bad. Perhaps on other days I would have been secure with the questions. But not this day.

The very idea of Evin, the horror of every Persian nightmare, was too much for my mind. I couldn't concentrate. Then, to top off, Ali showed me a letter from Esau. The letter said, "I can attest that this man, Yacoub Al-Tamimi, was a Muslim at birth, and that he has committed apostasy in converting to Christianity." The letter had all the wallop of a potential death sentence for apostasy. *How did Esau have the contacts to reach me with such a calamity here?*

Ali offered no solace, "You know what this letter can mean."

Ali had reached the core of my uncertainty. Not only was I now accused of being a Muslim apostate; and though I knew that was false, Ali had baited me into questioning the strength of my belief in the work of Jesus! *Why did I deserve Esau's accusation, and even more, the protection of Jesus' sacrifice?* I had been troubled in my spirit since I first left Kuwait for King's College, and now my fear doubled.

Ali acknowledged my limits and terminated that line of questioning. *Why was he testing my faith when I anticipated his main objective to be my incrimination?*

His demeanor changed when he turned to my friends who had disappeared, Abbas and Shaheen. He moved closer to me, his face directly in front of mine, with a wrinkle between his eyebrows. "We know all about these two. There is nothing more you can tell us. They were duly charged with apostasy, and the proper penalty administered. We want to know about the others." Now, the old questions again.

I experienced a surge of courage. "There were no others."

Ali left me in my cell without another word. He had demonstrated two lines of questioning – on the one hand, his questions had been focused on determining my spiritual condition, and on the other, in trying to uncover information about other believers. And then there was that praying callus on his forehead. I feared his return to ask more questions I couldn't answer.

For three days I was kept in my cell with no questioning. Food was brought twice a day, two dry pieces of flatbread in the morning and tea, rice, and beans in the evening, insects in the rice. I got brown water from my single tap. Ali had taken back the blanket with him. The uncertainty of when, or if, physical torture would begin was worse than the uncomfortable quarters. I was adrift, and couldn't sleep. *Did God have a plan in this?* Fear reigned.

Ali never came again.

By the fifth day, I was allowed to leave my cell for meals and one hour in the prison yard with other inmates. The yard was stark with no grass, only small, pointed stones that jabbed through my prison-issue, thin-soled shoes.

One of my prison mates was Omid Kokabee, who was taken captive after returning from an American graduate school to visit his family in Iran. Omid was a laser physicist. The government had offered to allow him to spend his sentence doing laboratory work on their weapons systems, but he had refused as a matter of conscience. He was a hero in the yard. How could he have had such courage? He was a secular Sunni Muslim and uninterested in religion. I tried to interest him in Christianity, but he was unmoved and turned away to talk with other inmates. "Don't bother me with that stuff."

I took this failure as God's sign to me. Psalm 86:1 says, "Incline your ear, O Lord, and answer me, for I am poor and needy." The psalm indicates the importance of admitting our destitute state. There was no question about the magnitude of my need, but I hadn't once voiced a prayer or thrown myself on God's mercy.

A short time later my physical and emotional torture began. I was transferred to Ward 350 for political prisoners. My new cell was smaller and there was no bed, just a sheet on the concrete floor, which drained the heat from my body when I tried to sleep. Sitting up was better. Three days each week they took me to a soundproof room and tortured me with electric shock and needles. The needles were inserted in my groin area, and the electric shocks were applied to my testicles. I screamed for so long that my voice disappeared. I wondered if the soundproofing was adequate to conceal my cries. The taller of my two tormentors, the one most adept in this method, kept repeating, "Perhaps you would like to tell us about those you brought into apostasy."

They also beat me with a small wooden club. Usually this was carried out by the shorter of the two, as he specialized in the use of this crude instrument. Welts arose on my sides and back, and the blood vessels under the skin ruptured. His comment: "It appears you're enjoying this. I'll try to make you even happier." The torture was designed not to leave any visible evidence outside the portion of my body covered by clothes. *How considerate.*

Another portion of the cruelty was even worse, the so-called *enferadi*, or white torture. I was confined in an isolation room with no communication whatsoever with others. The bright lights of the cell were kept on constantly with no break for sleep. Sometimes the lights flickered, only making the brightness more obvious. I tried everything to make the time pass – counting the blinks of my eyes, recalling long passages of my college textbooks, attempting to evoke dreams which previously had come so easily, and, of course, reciting the psalms. Nothing worked. Even when my eyes were closed, the white walls and white lights of the cell penetrated. I have no idea how long I was held in this solitary state. It did not take long before I did not have a sure sense of time at all. *Was it even passing? Would I ever see the sun or moon again? More than anything I longed for darkness and rest.* I began to lose myself in the interminable light.

Questionings, when they occurred, assumed a predictable course. "Why did you come to Iran? You're Kuwaiti. You came to disrupt our government and our citizens. Why do you despise us? We know your family is Christian and that you're Christian. Why did you leave Islam? You came to lead our citizens to apostasy, didn't you? We need to know the names of those you persuaded to apostasy." They all read from the same script.

Except for little Afsin, they already knew the answers to the last question. I assumed the others I led into apostasy, if I could even be credited with such a feat, were already dead. There was nothing for me to add. The guilt from my friends' deaths rested on me and hindered the little sleep I could get. After a while, I was ready to tell them anything, but I really had nothing to tell.

After a long time, they set up a video conference with my father and the rest of my family in Kuwait. It was a great relief to be around others in preparation for this. I was instructed to say I was well treated and make no mention of any charges. I obeyed, of course, just as I did for all their requests. The computer camera showed Papa, Hibah, and Binyamin sitting in our living room on the leather couch, all leaning forward, rigid, with their hands on their knees, all unaccustomed to this kind of communication. Binyamin was crying. The view was blurred, and papa's wrinkles were not clear. They carefully made no mention of the Kuwaiti Christian movement, and for that I was thankful.

There seemed to be no resolution in sight as the days in solitary and then later in being tortured continued. My urine showed blood, indicating kidney damage, and the physical cruelty was concluded for a time. Maybe they didn't want there to be any lasting proof. *Did that mean I would eventually be released?*

Once again my skill in simple accounting that had been so valuable at Kashan came to the fore. A guard informed me that the warden wanted to see me the next morning. I was allowed to go to the library for the first time when I told the guard it would help me do whatever was wanted. There I learned as much as I could about the man who held my fate in his hands. Copies of old newspapers in the otherwise pitiful prison library, told the story. Some time before, political prisoners had demanded to be present during a monthly search of their cells. In order to collect physical evidence against the prisoners, the prison guards took most of the prisoners' personal belongings. After that, the punishment for contraband ensued. Prisoners were blindfolded and handcuffed before being shoved through a gauntlet formed by security officials carrying batons. They were struck on their backs, heads and faces, and some were forced to strip naked before being locked in cells. That the prison had allowed this newspaper report to be available in the library sent us, the inmates, a clear message; its publication in the newspaper likely was designed to intimidate the general population.

This was the same warden I was to face: Ali Rashidi, who, along with his executive assistant, Java Moemeni, had supervised this newspaper-described assault on Ward 350 a year earlier – later called "Black Thursday." I was nauseous with fear. *What did he want from me?*

I expected the worst. Rashidi was a towering man whose bulk reminded me of a pyramid, the peak being his tiny, bald head. His eyes looked too big.

"Mr. Al-Tamimi, I have some requirements that cannot be met by my current staff. We have need of your skills. We've heard how you handled the finances at Kashan. Here at Evin I have a complex job for you, and we expect you to assist. This is not a choice."

"I understand. Will the torture stop?"

"Torture does not exist at Evin. We employ moral persuasion, which is designed to evoke your sense of humanity. You do not experience physical pain here." A plain lie, which he told with ease.

Try as I might, I could not fathom who was actually in control of the prison system in general and particularly, that of Evin. The funding emanated from the parliament, but the parliament was under the indirect control of the Council Guardians, half of whom were appointed by the Supreme Leader, the Ayatollah. The roles of the Islamic Revolutionary Guard Corps and the Ministry of Intelligence and Security were undoubtedly related in some way.

Rashidi took me to the accounting center which was much larger than the one at Kashan, recently painted, with newer computers, more windows, and two employees hard at work. They didn't look up as he passed. Rashidi dismissed them and told them to go home. They left shaking their heads; the government and their families' position guaranteed their jobs. As they departed, Rashidi said, "Don't worry, your monthly check will continue."

Rashidi gave me a complex plan. I was instructed to memorize it and not write it down. The plan was a shell game of finances designed to move the funds from three different pots: one from general government funding, one from the Revolutionary Guard, and the third from the Ministry of Intelligence. At each transfer of the funds, the money was to be placed in another internal account, present only on the Evin computer system. He told me to generate a password for this account. "Keep the password to yourself. I don't want to know it." I was more suspicious by the moment. Then, a fourth transfer of five percent of all the incoming funds would be made to an outside account, and the remainder put in the regular prison account for routine expenditures. I was given the routing number of the bank along with an account number to which the funds should be transferred. By moving the funds in this complex pattern, it would be difficult to determine if funds were lost at any one point. I was to determine the schedule of transfers in a non-repeating fashion and not inform Rashidi of the variations. Again, another cause for alarm.

The transfers quickly became routine for me. Compliance was an easy way to avoid beatings. Rashidi developed confidence in me, and soon we began to discuss personal issues. He was curious how I had become a Christian. He seemed a kind man, and I couldn't picture him as the author of the Ward 350 assault. I told him about my mother: how she used the Bible to teach herself to read, and eventually brought about the conversion of our entire family.

He finally divulged private information about his family and his only son who had thalassemia, a blood disorder causing severe anemia, which he was unlikely to survive. "I've tried to get treatment for my son here in Iran. Nothing has helped. He receives transfusions every week, and gets sicker with every procedure. He cries from the pain, and has developed antibodies against the transfused blood, which make it difficult even to proceed. His face has become deformed because there's compensatory bone marrow activity in his bones."

He opened the top drawer on this desk and showed me a photograph that was not displayed on his desk. *Was he ashamed of the child?* The little boy had a protuberant forehead and large, high cheekbones. His dark eyes protruded from their orbits and begged for forgiveness – for sins I speculated he had not yet committed. Rashidi was inconsolable as he disclosed his fears, crying at one point. He saw nothing but death for his son, and I saw a man concerned about his child.

The reason for the embezzlement of funds soon became clear. Rashidi was using them to provide the best possible medical care for his son. Still the care was not enough, and the boy's condition declined.

As part of my duties in the accounting office, I had access to e-mails, as long as I asked permission. The guard read the e-mails before they were sent. It was time to call on my old nemesis, Farmson, who had finally made it to medical school. I e-mailed him out of desperation. He replied, "Well, chum, you've got yourself in a mess now, just like we said you would."

After I asked him about treatment for thalassemia, he wrote me of a program, which was available at Great Ormond Street Hospital, where he was doing his pediatric rotation. The procedure involved stem cell transplants. The good news was that they would accept Rashidi's son for treatment, but for a considerable amount. They were always eager, he said, to get cash payment from patients coming from the Middle East.

Rashidi was elated. He instructed me to increase the fund transfers to ten percent.

Because of Rashidi's position, the treatment plan for his son became widely known. Rashidi was aghast when a cleric suggested the procedure might be against Islamic law. *And what's the religious reasoning on that one?* I wondered. Following a transfer from Rashidi's bank funds to the cleric, a convenient fatwa or Islamic ruling resolved that issue in the boy's favor. *Hmm.*

On January 8, 2016 Youness flew to London with his father. There the little boy underwent allogeneic hematopoietic stem cell transplantation, which means that a matched donor was located and the blood-making stem cells from the donor administered to the patient. The procedure had a high risk of failure and physical danger because it required that drugs first be administered to destroy the child's own defective bone marrow. I was stiff with fear. If that boy died with the treatment, I would be blamed. And then, nothing would save me.

Two months later Rashidi and his son returned home. The thalassemia was reversed, the anemia was relieved, and the father seemed suitably grateful. I hoped this happy outcome would lead to improvement in my status. This was my selfish thought about what was a life-saving, life-changing event for little Youness. Certainly the father's thankfulness was real; mine was motivated by my hope for safety.

Two weeks later before breakfast Rashidi himself came to my cell. My heart beat faster and I began to sweat at the novelty of his visit. He was pale and stiff. The Ministry of Intelligence were checking Evin's books. "Don't discuss this with anyone. Continue in your job. I think I can cover the matter." He didn't sound convinced, and his eyes were too wide and bulging.

As the funds had been transferred to Rashidi's account, I assumed I was safe. But after breakfast when I called the bank, I discovered my name had been inserted in the place of Rashidi's. No funds were left in the account. I had completely misread the man. This had been his plan from the beginning. How easily had I been taken in!

The Ministry of Intelligence wasted no time in my prosecution, and a court date was set the next week. As I was taken away to court, Rashidi smiled and said, "And what has Jesus done for you today?" I could now picture him as the stealthy instigator of the Ward 350 incident. He was far more devious than I had expected.

The prosecutor said, "You have no need for an attorney. Your guilt is certain. You have stolen from the Great Leader himself." Given the sequence of events and Rahsidi's cleverness, an attorney could have done nothing. The trial lasted less than an hour.

After the guilty verdict, I was left sitting in a holding cell for two hours, awaiting sentence. *Would they inflict the strict Islamic punishment for theft? Would they cut off my hand? Which hand?* I was right-handed. I hoped not the right hand. Perhaps I could learn to manage with no left hand. *What about the pain of amputation?* I was certain they would use no anesthetic.

The guards, one on each of my arms, brought me back to the courtroom. I was positive they could feel me shaking. When the judge pronounced the verdict of five years at Evin for embezzlement of the state funds, I was relieved. How great a blessing that I would not lose my hand. I was allowed to call my father and tell him about my sentence. I suppose in some way an official sentence was relief to us all.

Here I was back in Ward 350 again, now for five years more of enferadi.

###

But God intervened again. Rashidi came to my cell thirty minutes after the trial. "I want you to see how kind I am. You have a choice. You could remain here in your cell for the next five years. You must understand that may entail more of the physical trials to which you were formerly subjected, only worse. Or you may accept the government's generous offer, which I've arranged." He handed me a letter from the Organization for Investment Economic and Technical Assistance. It read:

"Dear Mr. Al-Tamimi,

We invite you to participate in a project, which is designed to enhance the world status of our great country. You will find the work in the Technical Assistance Organization to be very satisfying. We hope you accept our kind offer, and we welcome you as an honored guest.

Sincerely,

Mahmoud Rashidi"

Surely my assistance was not designed for good. I didn't know the assignment, but there was no way they were going to give me an honorable job. There were plenty of unemployed Persians for that sort of work. It had to be something underhanded. The Iranian government wanted a scapegoat to take the blame if illegal activity was discovered. That was to be me.

Unlike my colleague Kokabee, who had taken the high road, I didn't refuse. The thought of continuing in Evin for five years, with the on-again, off-again torture, was more than I could stand. Given the choice of working outside the prison, I could not decline. How could anyone choose Evin? How did Kokabee resist? His honorable choice was impossible for me. I could handle no more of Evin. There was no will left within me to refuse the offer.

CHAPTER 9

THE BOMB MAN

In Iran, the Organization for Investment Economic and Technical Assistance is an impenetrable institution affiliated with the Ministry of Economic Affairs and Finance. Their workings are purposely obscure even to their sister ministries. They operate under the Foreign Investment Promotion and Protection Act, which functions to provide legal cover, both transparent and opaque, to a variety of fund transfers and purchases. Now supported by thirteen countries, it is touted as the "New Silk Road of the Twenty-first Century." All foreign investments and purchases had to pass through this organization in Iran. My acceptance of the job thrust me into a secretive, and possibly malevolent, society. Such was my assignment.

News of the western New Year of 2016 bubbled with the international nuclear deal nearly concluded. The networks droned, each with a different view of the agreement. By mid-January Iran, after accepting a system of inspections and restrictions on its nuclear program, was to have many of its sanctions lifted and a huge amount of money, perhaps 150 billion dollars, returned from previously frozen accounts. Several of my prison mates at Evin were released in trade for Iranian citizens under U.S. prosecution. The goodbye was happy for them, but a sad affair for the rest of us. None of those released bothered to look back. They were freed as part of the settlement, while my sentence to work for the Iranian government would turn into a way for Iran to avoid the details of the pact they just made.

The very complexity of the façade of the Organization for Investment Economic and Technical Assistance made it capable of obscuring forbidden purchases from international view. Under Iran's current international agreements, which were designed to impede their nuclear program, the operation of this organization was essential for Iran's success in developing covert nuclear weapons. Was I to be the instrument of such an institution? *This is the job I accepted — anything to escape the torture of Evin.* One question tormented me: *Why did they choose me?* Surely there were qualified Iranian residents in need of such a job. Again, the only plan that made sense was that the government required a foreigner to blame if their plan went awry. So, there I was, offering myself up. *Fall guy extraordinaire.*

Assigned to a tiny apartment near the organization's headquarters on Davar Avenue in Tehran, I was awarded an allowance to purchase food. A black, uncomfortable, locked bracelet was affixed to my ankle with a tracking device and an alarm should I attempt to venture out of a two-block radius.

My skill set was deemed particularly suitable to negotiating international contracts with countries and groups lying outside the range of the nuclear weapons restrictions. My job, plainly put, was to circumvent the restrictions of the international agreement and obtain devices, basic materials, and technical information to enhance Iran's progress toward obtaining a nuclear weapon. I consented to do what Kokabee, the atheist, had refused. Never mind that I was a Christian.

I was assigned to the Researches and Foreign Economic Relations Office. It was no coincidence that Mahmoud Rashidi, my supervisor, was Ali Rashidi's brother, the only familial resemblance being his bulging eyes. One of the armed guards took me up to his office on the second floor and, after an hour on the hard bench in the waiting room wondering what I had done that warranted the delay, a sycophantic male secretary ushered me into Rashidi's oak-paneled office. Cigarette smoke hung in the room like a wreath, choking me. Several half glasses of tea, each containing an extinguished cigarette, sat on the desk. I expected to be offered tea but there was none for me. Rashidi did not look up for a full minute, but then he finally addressed me. "My brother told me about you. I hope your persuasive abilities are better than he indicated or you won't be up to the task. The help we need is critical to the country." I tried to lean back in the chair and appear confident but it didn't work. I couldn't stop fidgeting and blinking.

"You will first direct your attention to the work with the Pakistan Atomic Energy Commission. We want you to firm up our relationship with them. I can see by your expression you're distressed; and yes, you will be working for our country to procure a nuclear weapon." *So much for any hope of honest employment.*

137

The young men with whom I was engaged were disciples of Abdul Qadeer Khan, the father of Pakistan's nuclear program. Since I was not allowed to leave the country, we invited two of these men to Tehran for the introductory meeting. I was given considerable latitude to find out what they required in order to proceed with further business. We went to dinner within my two-block radius (I avoided telling them about my short leash), where I treated them to Iranian cuisine: pomegranate walnut stew, eggplant and tomato stew, and rice with dill and fava beans. The aroma emanating from the kitchen gave me confidence in my choice for the meal, which enhanced my newfound determination to be an engaging host. After all, in Middle Eastern culture, much more than in the West, personal relationships are the basis for successful deals. Failure would mean my return to imprisonment – no more of that for me.

"Yusef, I'm sure it's in your interest that our arrangements proceed without any delays along the way," said Latif, wolfing down his meal.

His partner, Abdul, added, "Yes, in the deals we have through with other groups, we've found that speed and efficiency overcome many deficiencies that could arise along the way. Delays can even cause projects to fail." I put down my fork. The fact that both brought up the same issue made me think we were getting to the point, their point of the meeting.

"I see you're anxious about this line of discussion," Latif continued, "but all the difficulties can be smoothed over by your making certain our time here is *personally* worthwhile."

"Yes, I'll see to that." I had to assume Rashidi expected bribes. The meal went smoothly after that. I would be sure to meet their needs.

I was only a financial expert. I had no knowledge of what sort of goods Iran needed to proceed. A trip to the processing facility in Natanz would be necessary, so our guests could see the status of our nuclear facilities for themselves. With secret service protection, I accompanied them, delighted to get out of Tehran, even on a nuclear tether.

After a long ride, avoiding any talk of bribes in the presence of the driver, we arrived. The gate guards swept the undercarriage of our Mercedes with mirrors, looked us over as unfamiliar, and perused our papers for ten minutes. After a call to their supervisor, we were finally admitted.

The building was a cubic four-story white concrete building with only a scattering of windows. My guess was that it had been designed to look as boring as possible. We were admitted through the front door security and given thick, weighty, white garb to put on over our clothes. We were then taken through hall after hall containing large, tube-shaped structures, metal vessels, and arrays of dials and gauges. I had no idea what I was seeing. Abdul and Latif shook their heads in feigned dismay and smiled at each other as they surveyed the facility. "We had no idea you were so far behind." Sales pitch lesson number one demonstrated. It was soon clear from their comments that Iran's needs were immense if a weapon was to be produced within a year.

Pakistan promised full cooperation, just as they had in assisting North Korea. *How could I do this to the rest of the Gulf? And what about Israel?* My mother would have brought up Israel the first thing. Was there any chance of my withdrawing at this point? Not without a return to Evin.

I quickly learned the basics of bomb construction. Our visitors smiled again at each other as they made a list of what we needed. They anticipated a substantial reward. The most important item on the list was fissionable material. The main ingredient we did not possess was an adequate amount of uranium 235, which must be prepared from uranium 238. The uranium 235 required separation in a centrifugal system linked together so as to produce a series of increasing uranium 235 concentrations up to the necessary ninety percent enrichment. The main choice we had to make was whether we should purchase the already enriched uranium or the necessary centrifugal equipment to continue the process on our own. Although we already had centrifuges, they were not adequate for the job. Many centrifuges had already been sacrificed as part of the new international deal. As I anticipated, Iranian officials wanted to be able to make their own, so the centrifuges were on the list. The price of this additional equipment? Two billion U.S. dollars.

The second requirement after the enriched uranium 235 was a detonation system. The simplest method, the two informed me, was to use conventional explosives surrounding the nuclear core material to produce a blast, which then initiated the nuclear reaction at the core. They recommended we utilize the improved method of two-point implosion. The Pakistanis advocated Semtex, an odorless, plastic explosive. The detonator itself was essentially an electronic device used to ignite the Semtex. The Pakistani team offered to sell us a complete detonation system for 2 million U.S. dollars for each separate bomb module. We purchased ten. I tried to shake the pride in being involved in such an historically significant project. What a ridiculous feeling – success, betrayal, and self-preservation, all wrapped into one package.

The Pakistani team agreed to return and give on-site instruction when we reached the point of assembly. Thus, the total cost for the equipment was two billion dollars plus twenty million dollars. For their personal assistance the visitors requested a five percent private service fee, which they agreed to round off to 100 million dollars. I phoned Rashidi about the costs. He was not put off. "Sounds routine."

Abdul and Latif, our highly skilled consultants, flew back by private jet to Lahore, and I rode back to Tehran in the same Mercedes. My drivers took me on a side trip to the planned bomb assembly site, one not on the international inspection list. It had already been prepared underground in the Bafq Protected Area, a rugged, arid land of barren rocks and hills. The area was a wilderness of sandy, arid, near-desert stark beauty. It was a vacation day for me, and I was encouraged to see such a beautiful example of God's work, even in a landscape as forbidding as this one. The site was originally designed as a national wildlife refuge and contained rare Asian cheetahs, leopards, gazelles, wild sheep and goats, wild cats, jackals, and rare birds. A gazelle wandered in front of our car, and I gasped as we just missed the graceful creature. No cheetah or gazelle would dare betray the secret. Rashidi, whom I now recognized as having a sense of humor, had named this project Operation Cheetah.

When I arrived back in Tehran, I informed Rashidi of the details. He presented the numbers to the Organization for Investment, and they accepted the proposal without disagreement. He said, "Yusef, your service to Iran will always be remembered." Hardly reassured by this statement, I hoped it was a lie. *Was there an information pipeline to Esau here too?* From the previous communications, I knew there was.

The next concern was the delivery process. The Chinese were the obvious choice here. For many years they had been selling missiles capable of delivering nuclear devices. Their standard charge was 10.5 million dollars per unit. We purchased ten.

The final component of the program, which would need to be ongoing, involved the fitting of nuclear explosives to the missile. For this task we needed several consultants who would remain on-site for assembly. The North Koreans were quite helpful in this regard, and they had unexpected knowledge about miniaturization of the bomb payload. Compared to the already expended funds, their cost was minimal. They worked cheap, no bribes required, with all the funds immediately sent by wire transfer to the North Korean government.

And so, I obtained nuclear weapons for Iran. That I had done so, solely for my own protection, sent a foul odor up to God. I could smell it too. Would the weapons be used?

This whole time Western inspectors continued their work dutifully in areas where no nuclear weapons would be discovered. The inspections and monitoring proceeded according to the new agreement. Its enforcement was monitoring the percentage of uranium 235 produced by the centrifuges at Fordow, Lashkar Abad, and Natanz. The inspectors stuck to the rules of the arrangement and went only where they were allowed. Both sides knew no weapons would be found. The agreement was designed to have a favorable outcome for all — with no bad news attached. Since we had purchased the necessary materials and equipment to proceed with rapid processing of uranium, the deal with the Western powers had no real meaning other than political subterfuge for both sides. Although the West did not know the specifics, they were not naïve to the Iranian intent to achieve nuclear capability. *Surely the Americans must know.* That thought salved my conscience. *Would they know about me?* I was a small fish. And besides, Donald Trump had just been elected president in the U.S., and no one knew what was next from the angry American cowboy. Perhaps his intentions were even less holy than mine.

The last step for completing the negotiated deals was the creation of written contracts for the transfer of funds, which would be subject to evaluation outside the ministry and perhaps by Western reviewers. This arrangement was part of the agreement with the U.S. and their allies, that all large international purchases required external examination. The contracts I put together to cover our nuclear acquisitions appeared to be for the purchase of sophisticated agricultural techniques and equipment. Rashidi was completely enthralled with the job I had done in the short span of six weeks.

How could I have been so effective in the face of moral disaster? It would take another year, and perhaps well into 2017, for the nuclear weapons to be ready for testing or for use. Testing was probably not necessary, as the Pakistanis and North Koreans had given their guarantees. Deliveries occurred at the port of Bandar Abbas near the Strait of Hormuz where the materials were off-loaded from South African registered vessels and transported by truck to the Bafq Protected Area. The trucks were marked as agricultural companies, covering the weapon materials stuffed within. All transfers occurred on moonless nights to avoid detection by American satellites. I had outsmarted all the outside observers, but my success hung over me like a guillotine.

I hoped the weapons would never be tested. For Iran to do so would make a mockery of the treaty with the West, and their discovery might eventually point to me. I wondered what the value of the weapons really was to Iran. If no one knows you have the weapons, they have no effect. They are neither offensive nor defensive. But those I worked for were satisfied. *Perhaps they intended to use the weapons in a surprise attack*, an awful thought. As a reward for my success, the radius on my ankle bracelet was increased to four blocks.

###

Just as I thought the worst was over and that I could survive comfortably for the remaining four and one half years of my term, another layer of misery was added. I knew now I was trapped. Even though I had computer access, I couldn't ask for outside help, not through an international news sources or Amnesty International or the Kuwaiti consulate, or any such group. Now that I had assisted in Iran's nuclear weapon program, I could be considered an international criminal. And Esau surely possessed this knowledge. He was everywhere.

Rashidi's kindness in increasing my fetter was reversed and the radius of my electronic ankle bracelet was shortened to only one block. They were masterful in keeping me off-balance. I had no idea why they pulled back on the rewards I anticipated after the success of Operation Cheetah. Not only did they control my physical state, they managed my emotions too. I was subjected to daily questioning for four hours in what seemed a pointlessly cruel manner. Some days the four hours were in the morning, sometimes the afternoon, but the most troublesome were the ones that extended into the night or early morning hours. I was still expected to complete all aspects of my job.

###

One day I received a written message: "I know what you're doing. Congratulations!" It was from Esau. His knowledge still startled me. Was this an escalation of his involvement?

###

145

And then there were the events in Qatar, as they were accused of collaboration with Iran. Saudi Arabia, the United Arab Emirates, Egypt, and Bahrain had embargoed Qatar because of their suspicions. Who had arranged such collaborations between Iran and Qatar? The news filtered out to me. Once again, there was Esau. His interactions were unending.

In the midst of the work and the endless questioning, strangely timed, my father was given a visa and came to Tehran to see me. He stayed with me in my small apartment for two days and I was allowed a respite from the questioning.

But there was no relief from the pressure of my confinement. My apartment was bugged by my captors. A knock on my door prior to my father's arrival opened to two technicians with brown cases of electronic equipment. "We must know everything that is said here. Don't touch the microphones, or there will be a penalty, one you won't like." They were efficient, kind, and unapologetic.

My father was now an old man of 78. In the time since I had previously seen him, his physical condition had visibly deteriorated, and he walked with a cane and in evident pain, but his mind was quick and his thoughts tuned to the Lord. "Yusef, you must know God is in charge of all you're going through." He was more peaceful and settled than I had ever seen him. Even my apartment prison didn't upset him. Our conversation was unaltered by the bugs we both knew were in operation. "We can say whatever we wish. What can we hide at this point?" Indeed there were no secrets left.

I knew he was worried about my physical situation, but then came the key comment. "What's happening with your spirit? You seem without an anchor." He was right, and I had no response.

Still, he was calm and confident, for reasons I didn't yet understand. My mother on whom he depended had been dead for many years. He had recuperated from the loss to the best extent possible. When he spoke of her, he smiled. "She was a saint." And of course, she was.

I was allowed to take my father to dinner at a restaurant outside my usual radius. We passed by the Fountain of the Martyrs, which commemorated those who died in the Iran-Iraq war. Colored red water spewed from the fountain, suggesting the blood of the sufferers. Such was the tasteless rendering by the upper level clergy.

We arrived at Nayeb, a restaurant festooned in browns and yellows, where I ordered jeweled rice, a dish with carrots, sugar, saffron, oranges, and dried fruit followed by *zereshk polo ba morgh* (barberry rice with chicken). My father didn't like my choice. The mix of spices was so unlike Kuwaiti fare, and I felt I had spoiled the evening with my departure from the plain, sturdy taste of our Kuwaiti chicken dishes. But the food was not the main issue. Our mutual feelings of dismay over my situation were the chief source of the damage. He was sad for my lagging spirit, and I was despondent over my guilt and loss of freedom.

My ankle bracelet was also decorated with a listening device, and the restaurant provided no shelter from my omnipresent watchdogs. I told him the story of how I arrived at my present job, as well as how I had been manipulated by Rashidi at Evin prison. For a while I stopped there, but I couldn't hold back. I proceeded to tell him of the nuclear project and how I had helped. I had to be honest with him. "Papa, you can't tell anyone in Kuwait about this. If it becomes known, I'll be charged in the international court when I'm released from prison here. Esau could do this."

"Yusef, I've been so worried about you. And now, with what you've told me, I can see it is worse than I thought. I can't imagine what you're going through. I don't know how they've forced you to do all that you've told me about. You still have four years to go. How will it be for you when this is over?"

I shook my head, and replied, "I don't know, Papa. The Lord must have a plan for this, but I don't see it."

"I don't see it either. I'm not sure I'll ever see you again, and I don't want it to finish with this – your endless imprisonment. I came to encourage you, and I feel like I'm unable to help. All I can tell you is this: I've been in places in my life where I saw no exit. And somehow…" His voice trailed off for a moment. "I remember you from the time you were born. You were beautiful. There were none as handsome, none as charming as you. The Lord blessed you with gifts designed for greatness. You still possess those gifts. We have to base our hope on what the Lord has done in the past. He will never forsake us, no matter what."

His comment seemed empty to me. I had made choices, and

they hadn't been good ones. I was thankful my father didn't discuss the nuclear weapons issue and the disasters that could arise from it. I understood what he was saying to me, but my heart just could not grasp the hope he was trying to share. I felt I had gone too far.

We talked the remainder of the time about events in Kuwait. I learned that my half-brother Thawab had expressed belief in Jesus. The government had taken no action against him, but several Muslims had decided to correct Thawab's apostasy, and they had attacked him with swords. He had been hospitalized at Mubarak in intensive care for three weeks.

My father continued. The number of Kuwaiti Christians had grown substantially. Most sought to conceal their conversion by taking their worship of Jesus to the mosque. Those with more courage formed house churches. "The government doesn't know how to deal with us. If they raise the issue publicly, then it would rise to the level of controversy in the community. And Kuwait wants no such controversy. The government still operates with the goal of self-preservation at the cost of principle."

I asked, "What about dreams?" I brought up dreams because they had been the bright side of my sojourn so far. The evening needed a bright side.

My father smiled, "The dreams don't amount to much in Kuwait. The gospel has grown by the more usual method: person-to-person."

Finally, my father told me about my half-brother, Esau. "He's taken a new position in Kuwait as a computer programmer at Al-Bader Trading Company. He prosecutes the cause of Islam by any means he can. As we suspected, he's definitely been identified with extremist groups. We know he's in charge of e-mail hacking as a tool to find Christians. With his obvious al-Qaeda or ISIL affiliations, Esau's path will only get worse." I knew Esau had contacts in Iran, but their nature was unclear to me. *Was he orchestrating my detention?* And the religious confusion: *How was he stirring the pot with both Sunni and Shia elements?*

We both thought we were unlikely to see each other again, and the visit had been a rather sad one, not greatly uplifting for either of us. I was thankful my father had not been critical of my cowardice. He only said, "You're too much like me. You're careful, not brave. I love you, no matter what. How can I tell of what you've done here when I can't reveal all I've done?" With that very real reassurance, he embraced me as I put him in a taxi for the airport. Surely this meeting was our last on earth.

After my father's departure, my painful schedule resumed and showed no sign of stopping. A series of questioners took on the challenge of breaking me down, but there was no place left that had not already been broken. They might have succeeded if I knew what they wanted, but their questions made no sense to me. I would have been glad to tell them anything useful to get them to stop. Everything except Afsin. "Why did you become a Christian? Who are your friends? Who gave you money? How did you get a job in Iran?" I should have been encouraged by the lack of depth in their questions. But I didn't think of that at the time. The rosy future I had built in my imagination so long ago had been completely eradicated, leaving nothing except dread for the future and disappointment over the past.

The same set of questions were asked and answered over and over again until January 2018. Three full years still remained in my sentence.

CHAPTER 10

NEW DREAMS

Even in the midst of this vile routine and constant sleep deprivation, my dreams renewed in a kaleidoscopic fashion. At first the dreams rescued me, as they led to business successes, and my reputation blossomed.

In my waking hours, the interrogations stopped and my electronic tether was increased to an eight-block radius. As long as I didn't attempt to leave the country, I was essentially free. I was promoted for my ability, just as always, and I felt a slight, but temporary release from my bomb guilt.

It was then that a new dream, one that recurred many times, intervened. Its interpretation escaped me. The dream was delivered not to me but to the head of the Ministry of Economic Affairs and Finance, Karim Khadim. He brought me into his office and related his dream many times, the repetition reflecting his concern. "In the dream I see myself astride a white horse surveying a vast field of wheat. The field bears a sign: By This Field Your Debts Are Secured. Then the dream changes suddenly, and I find myself riding a black, gaunt mule in the midst of the same field, while grasshoppers devastate the field." He stopped for a moment and then continued, "If I had this dream only once, I wouldn't have thought

153

much of it, but I've had it frequently. The changes in it frighten me." Why was he being so frank, so self-abasing with me?

The idea of the loss of wealth was clear in Khadim's dream, but the addition of the concept of secured debt was more difficult. The fact that the dream was repeated showed that it was important and had the potential for some kind of widespread economic disruption. I was apprehensive, and my mind jumped from possibility to possibility.

But at this point my analysis of the dream failed. "Sir, I know the dream is about finances and some sort of economic disaster, but I don't know what to make of the message behind it." He kept asking me the same questions over and over. He was afraid, and I was now the focus. The finances were his responsibility. My obligation was to give answers to dreams. First the bomb guilt, and now this.

"Yusef, if you know what's good for you, you'd better get this right." Khadim urged. He was losing confidence in me. I imagined he thought my lack of a solution was due to a reluctance on my part to help him. He kept me running back and forth between my office and his, every time suggesting different possibilities. He dishonored himself by his anxiety and by coming to my office, but he was afraid of the consequences if he failed.

The unpleasantness of my incarceration resumed. My travel range was again restricted to one block. There were extended sessions of questioning without pattern, and once more, the sleep deprivation. Khadim turned up the pressure as his own anxiety increased.

I was certain the answer would come to me. Answers always had in the past, but weeks went by and nothing. I phoned my father. Knowing others were listening, I stated, "Papa, I know the answer to the dream will come to me, but I can't wait much longer."

"I don't know what to tell you. I realize you're on your own there. I'd help if I could. We're praying."

Why wouldn't God answer? Was this punishment for my role in the bomb? Had I considered all the options? No, no way, there had to be an answer.

For the first time in my life what I thought was my great gift of dream interpretation failed me. I was completely stumped. Humbled, I realized God bestowed His gifts at His pleasure; it was not mine. It had never been mine, which meant it was not to be used for my fame either. Khadim stopped speaking to me, and my reputation shrank. My biblical namesake had succeeded at a similar juncture. Not me. Pharaoh lost his respect for me. I began to pray more earnestly than before.

Then the threats began, subtle at first. Khadim called me to his office. "I'm very sad for you. If this dream is important, and you haven't provided the answers, then the outcome of your time here could change." He averted his gaze and looked at his papers on the desk before him.

"I don't understand. What could change?" *Where were we head-*

ed with this discussion?

"You must know that nothing in Iran is ever completely set-tled." He dropped the line of discussion and moved on.

What did he mean? Surely not a change in my sentence.

A subsequent conversation made it clearer. "Yusef, your sentence was given in the Public Court of the first level. I understand there are inquiries from the Court of Cassation about your sentence, and we have received new information from Kuwait that is quite telling." *Esau again?* Khadim looked at me directly and folded his arms across his chest. *Was he angry, simply stating the facts, or just using fear as his weapon?*

I recalled the incident of Majid Nafisi, when I had predicted his sentence would be changed to death, and the prediction came true. *What new sentence would they impose on me– more time, the amputation I feared, death?* My interpretation gift no longer served me. Now I was agitated, not only about the finances of Iran and Khadim's dream, but also my future. *God, please help me. I need You!*

A day later I received an e-mail from my younger brother, Binyamin. It was passed to me by the ever-present security. It was not unusual for me to hear from him. Binyamin and I had become increasingly close over our brief time together in Kuwait. He had advanced in maturity with great speed, and while there was a size-able gap in our ages, we were devoted to one another, just as I was with Hibah. I had missed hearing from him while incarcerated. At fifteen his technical skills were remarkable; he could hack into critical systems.

Binyamin, addressed me as "Dear Brother." He must have known others would read any correspondence first, so he didn't mention Esau by name, but I presumed he had somehow reached into Esau's computer system. What Binyamin conveyed was startling and gave me an immediate solution to the dream. An unnamed principle (Esau, of course) was frantically disposing of his company's position in the bond market. Associates in al-Qaeda and ISIL were initiating a run on the bond market, which was much more fragile than generally thought. Binyamin wrote, "Our father told us about your current distress. I think you must act on this information as soon as possible."

Of course! That was it! A thunderclap surely! But why had not Esau informed his contacts in Iran, the ones he must have. *Why was he holding out on them? How many sides could he play?*

My brother had discovered the key. *Why had I not figured this out for myself, even without God's help?* My interpretive gift had failed, but my brother's skill saved me. Actually, God had worked through my little brother to help me, but I did not give Him credit for what transpired. The small bit of humility I had shriveled like a prune.

The matter of secured debt was the crux of the matter. The world economy looked strong, the U.S. boom continued, and Europe was finally coming out of its long economic slowdown. China seemed to have gotten a handle on their strongly controlled, planned economy. Corruption had been reduced, or so they said.

However, in the midst of all this apparent prosperity, the debt capacity of world markets had been exceeded. The Chinese had concealed their deficiencies. In all the major states, debt was not really secured in any substantive way. I had not studied the bond market with the same thoroughness I pursued other financial areas, but a quick two-day study period led me to the same conclusions that had been reached by al-Qaeda and ISIL. Not only were corporate bonds approaching default, the same was true of municipalities and the short-term projects they were attempting to fund. Others would surely reach the same conclusion.

In order to maintain the attractiveness of bond-based borrowing in combination with the increased risk, the interest rates offered would have to rise. As a consequence, the value of bonds would fall. The bond market disaster could be triggered by a few payment defaults, which would occur first for those with lesser means to obscure the deficit. But the others would follow.

I hurried to Khadim's office and rushed past the secretary, who extended an arm to delay me. I was stronger than I had been in days. "Sir, I know the answer. The answer is a coming disaster in the bond market." I made recommendations to Khadim based on my assessment. My pronouncements destroyed his confidence in the bond market he relied upon. "The country should divest itself of all bond holdings immediately." Now I was giving him instructions. "You must take this action right away, but in an orderly manner, so as not to hasten a run on the market. After that, hold the resulting funds in escrow in gold reserves and do not reinvest them until the markets stabilize."

My excited and certain manner rattled him. I had not expressed such confidence in the past. He rose from his desk with me still in the room, something he never did. He was always one to maintain his edge of superiority outwardly. He paced as he talked through the best way to present the issue. "Wait here, Yusef," he commanded me. Khadim marched out to pass my recommendations up the line as his own, without mentioning their source. I didn't expect anything else. Only if it were proved wrong would the advice be laid at my door.

He must have had trouble convincing his superiors because Khadim did not return for two long hours. I waited. Their response was incomplete and slow. Why should they adopt such a ridiculous story? No other nation's leaders would have swallowed the same information in one bite. What should have taken three to six months was stretched by design to one year. But the slow pace was another triumph for Khadim. He took advantage of the casual pace and ordered me to divert one percent of the bond sales into his private account. In order to protect myself, I kept careful private records, tracking the funds. I knew that would do little good for me now, but perhaps there would come a time. One never knew.

In August 2018 the collapse Binyamin had predicted ensued. Iran had disposed of half its bond holdings, and invested that money in gold bullion. Their remaining bonds became worthless, but Iran was ahead of the rest of the world in this game. Gold prices soared, and Khadim was a hero of the state. He called me into his office, leaning back in his chair with his hands behind his head. "Yusef, I thank you for your service in this matter, but I want to caution you. Don't tell anyone about the dream and how you solved it. I get the credit for this. If you try to take it, life will not go well for you." I understood this better than anything else. I got it.

Khadim was kind to me, without portioning out the glory. I never expected he would share anything with me, and I was not wrong. He pulled me into his office again, iterating the same message: "Yusef, don't ever share your role in this." He smiled and dismissed me. But thanks to him, the interrogations stopped and my ankle bracelet was set to a 12-block radius, which greatly increased my social interaction.

Khadim was awarded more authority, and he took me up the line with him. The complex interaction of the ministry allowed considerable latitude in job responsibilities, and he was placed in charge of an amazing sum of funds. In point of fact, his duties exceeded his abilities. Only because of my skills in financial management was he not swallowed by this new position. It would take several years before the world bond crisis moderated, and he needed my help navigating these shoals competently.

I soon forgot the Lord had bypassed my interpretation gift and delivered me from the dream puzzle by other means. I mentally assumed credit for my new successes. I had achieved this victory with my superior acumen. Conveniently, my part in the bomb was forgotten.

However, acquaintances I had in the coffeehouses were close

enough to tell me the truth and snap me back to reality in my boastings. In my discussions with others, I often shared how I worked in helping to maintain Iran's financial security, without, of course, ever mentioning my part in the recent bond crisis. "Yusef, you're not the one who controls anything, neither dreams, nor the market, nor the inner workings of world finances," they adjured. I listened but put the comments aside. *Were the events on the God-scale or the Yusef-scale?*

Suddenly there were an abundance of dreams. *Were they God's outpouring to the recipients or God's lessons and traps for me?* Now just as the job exceeded my boss's competency, God's actions exceeded my faith. Men from all levels and professions began to share their dreams with me. I became known as their sidewalk café receptacle of visions and aspirations, someone who was sympathetic and knowledgeable of these strange occurrences. My path through the coffeehouses of Tehran led me to academics, students, and upper level businessmen.

Recitations of dreams took remarkably similar patterns. In all of them, a man approached them in some way, and there were always features which identified the man as Jesus. Conversion did not immediately follow these dreams. The dreamers required additional information – the realization that they were sinners and could not pay their own penalties and that Jesus had sacrificed Himself to make that payment. Sometimes I delivered the message. At other times my new colleagues did so. I heard this request repeatedly: "I must have a Bible."

###

A local Christian pastor of the Assyrian Evangelical Church supplied these at risk to his own safety. He came to me in the coffee shop and parked himself between my friend and me. Awkward. "I'll get Bibles for you," he spoke earnestly. "There are always methods, ways to do this. And if security catches me, there are others from my congregation who'll help."

Had he seen the inside of Evin? Did he know what he was doing? Surely not. But I accepted his help and failed to warn him because I was selfish for his assistance.

An added danger was the recent addition of surveillance cameras at all the coffeehouses. Our initial impression was that the cameras were for restaurant security, but the rumor spread that the state was actually using them to monitor what occurred in the establishments. We looked up at the cameras, and they looked down on us.

Thus, the conversations and particularly the transfer of Bibles had to be handled with care. One such transfer went awry. The young man with me, Abdul, pulled a Bible from under his coat and gave it to a new believer. It was too warm for such a heavy coat. I suppose this aroused their suspicions, and it was a full-sized book, too large for a clandestine transfer. An agent from the Ministry of Intelligence and Security appeared out of an unobtrusive door, one we had not even noticed, where he had been watching us. Knocking over coffee as he came, he put his hand on Abdul's shoulder. "What was that book?"

Abdul told the truth. There was no point in lying as the Bible was now in the hands of the new believer. "I just gave it to him as a present."

"You can't give Bibles to Muslims."

The new believer said, "I'm a Christian."

"You both come with me. Is he involved?" The agent pointed to me.

Both Abdul and the new believer denied my involvement, and I made no effort to correct them. I never saw them again. The number of dream searchers declined for a time.

Esau's shadow still lurked behind each corner of the coffee shops. Why was the monitor watching us and not the other patrons? Was he responsible for the disappearance of Abdul and that new believer?

An inkling of this possibility dribbled out to me in a conversation with Khadim. As we discussed the financial matters of the day, he slipped in the comment: "Please guard yourself in your little coffee klatches." My jaw dropped as I pondered the comment.

"I don't understand."

"You understand. You have an enemy, who resides in Kuwait, with important contacts here, and he uses them in many areas. You know who I mean, your half-brother."

"Do you mean Thawab?" I tested the water.

"Don't be stupid. You know. This secret one colludes with those in Iran who are above even me." *Is this possible?* "And you must understand, he works to diminish us all. The current Qatari mess is there, in which the Saudis have singled them out as a rogue state, which they are not. You're only a foil in these little matters." And he added, "The same for me, but for some reason, he really has it out for you."

"And by the way, my young friend, I am having your ankle bracelet removed. Go wherever you wish except the airport, and remember, the imams watch over us all." As I left his office, he placed his right hand briefly over his heart, an indication of respect. *Was it sincere? Or another deception?*

CHAPTER 11

THE ATTACK

I was summoned to the Ferdowsi Grand Hotel for a meeting with Khadim and colleagues from the Ministry of Industry, Mine, and Trade.

There was Esau. He was in the lobby, on the red velvet couch with his legs crossed, dark brown suit, red beard. When I first saw him, he was already staring at me as I passed through the metal screening device at the front of the hotel. I had not seen Esau since the episode at my school twelve years earlier, and he was balding and had gained a paunch, the latter made more obvious by the absent tie. Though our encounter seemed accidental, I'm sure it was not. He kept his eyes on me as I walked into the restaurant. What was this al-Qaeda representative, this ISIS mongrel, doing in my city? While he had been responsible for long-distance meddling in my affairs, was he now here for a frontal assault?

Khadim and I went in for the meal, in which we were going over some minor contracts with an African firm. So boring, but I could think of nothing but Esau guarding the door. After two hours we finished. My stomach was full of wilted salad and my ears stuffed with British accents.

On the way out, I searched the lobby. He was gone. *Could the figure of Esau have been a cruel and threatening apparition, fabricated by my own culpable mind? Was he just a phantasm with no real substance? Was he even here? After all, wasn't I responsible for part, or even all, of this clutter in my head?* I heard or saw nothing new for two weeks.

He was waiting at my doorstep, sitting awkwardly on the floor and leaning against the wall. *He was really here in Iran.* How did he locate my apartment? "Well, brother, it's time we talked again." I nodded, helping him up from his awkward crouch. He followed me into my apartment. "For a prisoner of the Ayatollah, you've done well. I suppose our genetics counts for something."

I put the key in the lock and we entered. Esau took my cue and sat in the single padded chair. "Here we are, two brothers, and nothing else to do but talk about the future."

"And what is that future?" I started the teapot and got out the tea. It was ready quickly. Esau had already adopted the Persian method of tea consumption. He poured the first quantity into the saucer with the sugar and slurped through his lips. We were no longer teacher and student, and some neutral social interaction was necessary to open the conversation.

Esau then took the lead. "Yusef, let's go out for a walk." I knew he wanted to avoid the apartment bugs, so I obeyed.

"You must be wondering why I'm here in Iran. Here it is. This Sunni versus Shia thing, Saudi versus Iran, and Christians dirtying the mix – this is barbarism, the result only of religious fanaticism, and I'll employ the present conflict for my purpose. And you know my purpose."

"I'm not sure that I do. I thought you were simply against Christianity. Whose side are you on?"

"What do I care about Islam or any religion? I only attend the services to position myself so I can finish off all you religious bigots, Christian, or otherwise, whoever lurks behind a particular symbol, cross, or crescent."

How could he carry out such an objective? It was much broader than I had believed. *I thought it had just been about me. Why was he here in Iran?*

He went on. "I want you to know I'm serious, that there'll be no mercy afforded to you or our family. You may wonder why I've bothered coming here. Well, it's my way of enjoying my vendetta." And then with no other word, he disappeared around the corner.

For another two weeks, there was nothing. Again, Esau had disappeared.

The citizen riots and uprisings over the failing Iranian economy had smoldered off and on all of 2018, and, because of their lack

167

of focus, had failed to achieve any real result. But as 2019 began, Esau put his plan into motion. I couldn't see it at first, but then…

The riots took on a fresh character, and rumors spread that Sunni fundamentalist elements were promoting the uprisings. I'd had enough of the Ayatollah nonsense and his secret service dealings, and now, it seemed, ISIL/al-Qaeda was being superimposed on the fomenting rebellion. On my way to work, men dressed in black with body armor and clubs blocked the street. They beat demonstrators, even if they were standing peacefully; blood stained the streets. Photographers were taken prisoner, their cameras confiscated. My colleagues in the ministry said this was the largest disturbance they had ever observed in Iran, even greater than the 2009 Green Rebellion. Everyone I knew was too young to recall the demonstrations against the Shah in 1979.

I tried to think through the instigating forces. My reasoning was bound by my long-term view of Iran – the inherent vitality and diversity of its people. The Ayatollah and his crowd had controlled the populace for too long with their ridiculous conservatism. Unfortunately, the regime had proven itself as corrupt as the one preceding it as they lined their pockets above all else. That deadly combination had choked the people and their individuality, and now the dam had burst. Or so I thought.

But there was more. The state-controlled news wouldn't admit to the invasion by Sunni elements, but the BBC reported that ISIL had taken credit for the civil disorder. That news spread through the populace. The word on the street was confused. Had they been taken advantage of? Should the protests continue?

Then there was *Al-Jazeera*, the Qatari station beamed in by the satellite dish on my roof; the station always brought a fresh, clear message. There she was in my living room again reporting on the civil disruption in the streets of Tehran: Tahara, her dark hair uncovered, and deep brown eyes staring intently into the camera, as if she were intentionally looking right at me. She had not left my mind since I had first seen her face when I was still free in Isfahan. I felt like she was speaking only to me, although we had never met. It was frustrating. I could never be near her. A silly, lingering crush.

The immediate provocation for the trouble on the streets, however, remained economic. The promised monetary windfall for Iran that had been made based on the July 2015 nuclear agreement had not come to fruition. The poor remained poor, and those without jobs still had none. Well-educated young people were idle and vented their frustrations in the street.

There were genuine, serious reasons for these "civil disturbances" (the controlled news refused to call it a revolt, which it was). My observations, based on my reading of the histories of other countries where these kinds of things had happened, told me that such unrest persisted for a while, ran its course, and weakened with the movement's failure to change anything. Fatigued, protestors lost their zeal for the cause, and limped off to a nearby corner to lick their wounds.

But this didn't occur. There were waves of violence, which flagged, but they were always renewed, as if by an infusion of energy. And the source of the energy, I found, was Esau and his connections.

Esau phoned me. He seemed to know or suspect that my phone was monitored by the ministry, or by other combatants, so he mentioned no specifics. "Meet me at that repulsive café on the corner tonight at 8:30." I felt that I had no choice but comply. I was haunted by the possibility that he had those above me in his pocket.

I was there at 8:15 and waited until 9 p.m., when Esau finally showed. He smiled at the fact I had stayed well past the appointed time. "Afraid to leave, eh? Very wise." He sat facing away from the ever-present security camera, smiling. "I suppose you want to hear the story of the Ayatollah's demise and how I've arranged it." *Inflated doggerel? Perhaps, but threatening nevertheless.* But still the Ayatollah remained in charge. I became distraught at the sight of Esau's red hair and powerful arms; this felt like a repetitive scene from *Groundhog Day.*

I sat with nothing to say, but Esau said plenty. "Here it is, my dear little brother. My contacts with the ISIL and al-Qaeda are quite helpful, and their objective is the same as mine. They are as anti-religious as I — that you must have known; and we will grant no more quarter. It's death to Islam. Death to Christianity and Christians. And I know how this will be achieved. The one who controls the money and the bomb will win, and that's me. Let's see some expression on your face. I can't stand your impassive

170

demeanor." I could only twist in my seat and wonder what was coming next – the bomb again? I had tried to forget.

"Here it is, little brother: You acquired bombs for this country, and they are very pretty, especially the one we have in safekeeping. That one is particularly attractive."

My mind jumped to my own safety. *How had Esau learned of my role? Did his connections have no bounds? They had to stop somewhere. But how did he possess one of the bombs?*

But then, finally, the greater problem hit me. *What did he intend to do with his bomb?*

And what should I do? Should I inform those above me about the danger? Who among them could I trust? What was the greater risk – that the bomb would actually be used, or that, by revealing the plot, I would place myself at risk for my role in obtaining them in the first place?

I concluded that the latter was the greater risk for me. *Surely, Esau and his henchmen wouldn't explode a nuclear bomb in Tehran. The bomb had more value as a threat.* More reasoning on my part without evidence.

I sat deadpan, making an effort to appear unimpressed. I observed the dissatisfaction in Esau's face, a blank expression, pallor increasing. Was he disappointed at my insufficient reaction? I summoned the waiter and ordered two Turkish coffees. "Let's talk further. Surely, there must be some common ground, some hope for resolution."

The evening waned, and the café emptied. Likely Esau saw the diminishing crowd as a disappearance of his cover for our meeting, because he drew the conversation to a close. "You get the idea, young man. There's destruction on the horizon, and you're responsible for it. I'm done talking with you." Abruptly, he pushed his coffee away, got up from the cast iron seat, and disappeared into the crowd.

CHAPTER 12

THE GAME

What happens next? What did I want to happen? What outcome would serve me best? Once more there was a long pause from Esau that left me without mooring, no fresh information. First and surprisingly to me, the riots continued. They did not peter out like most citizen-sponsored upheavals. I still wondered how Esau was connected to them though.

Rumors circulated in the ministry, and people started avoiding me. *Did they think I was connected to the unrest in the streets?* Khadim himself shifted his gaze away from me whenever I entered the room, and stopped speaking to me when others were around. For some reason, I was marked. *Or did I imagine this?*

I scoured the Tehran newspapers, including *Abrar, Khabar, Kayhan* (its editor appointed by the Ayatollah himself), and *Entemand Daily*, a paper reflecting the reformist view, for hints about the source and progress of the civil strife. The articles were sterile in their content, any real news mopped up by the state machinery. The papers blamed the United States for interfering in the nation's politics, though no such mechanism was documented as far as I knew. No ISIL/al-Qaeda connection was ever mentioned.

###

Then, on February 15, 2019 Esau tracked me down for a meeting at the same café. The temperature was 50 °F, and there few other patrons sitting along the sidewalk. Esau said the closed circuit camera was off, and he sat down hard in the metal chair and pulled up to the table, both elbows resting upon it so that his clasped hands were six inches from my face. *How could he know the surveillance camera was turned off?*

For a moment, just an instant, the thought came over me that this man in front of me, the one who had kicked me out of secondary school, the one who had declared himself an enemy to me and my family, was still my brother, and that I should feel something for him. The wrinkles in his face, the skin too fair for one native to the Middle East, evoked an emotion in me for the man. I had not experienced this before. Then, it was gone. It was as if he saw my thought because he smiled before he began.

"I'm sure you're puzzled by recent events, and you must want to know what's really happening." *Yup.* "I hope this interval has whetted your appetite. Now, I'm going to bring you into the script to a degree you will not enjoy."

Even though I wanted to know what was going on – about the riots, the bomb, and his ISIL/al-Qaeda connection, if there was one, to know any of this was potentially unsafe.

"Ok, Yusef, here it is." He put his palms down on the tabletop as if he was preparing to place his bets at a roulette table. "ISIL and al-Qaeda have joined forces. ISIL ran out of money when they lost the oil-producing territory in Iraq and Syria, and they had no choice but to join al-Qaeda, which still gets their financial support from the Saudis." Most observers had suspected as much. "I'm using their people here in Tehran to undermine the religious authorities in the government. Riots occur as I decree." I couldn't believe this was happening under my nose, and that I was now caught up in the plot. Esau knew that if I reported what he was doing, I would be considered a collaborator. I could only sit and watch.

I returned to my government-provided apartment, more paranoid than ever. *Was I being watched to an even greater degree than usual?* I closed the ragged curtains on my window, turned on the lamp next to my lumpy chair in front of the TV, and switched on IRIB TV2, the station operated by the Islamic Republic. The news was on. The "public displeasure" as it was called, was mentioned briefly, with no photos. Out in the street under my window, the drums thumped incessantly, and marchers chanted "Death to the Ayatollah." Gazing from my window, I could see that the armor-clad police did little to stop them. But looking closer I saw them – the guarantors of the disturbance – a component I had missed before. Large, thick-shouldered men with full beards in black leather jackets had positioned themselves at quadrants around the crowd. When participants in the disturbance attempted to leave, they were gently but firmly urged back into the moving mass.

How had this happened? How had ISIL/al-Qaeda goons been allowed this power? Now, I saw that Esau's words as accurate. Where were the vaunted Revolutionary Guards and their civilian counterparts, the Basij? I could think of only one way they could be controlled: an infusion of money into their pockets. The Ayatollah and his like must be fuming over the failure of their minions to control this situation. *How could Esau have such funds under his control? From the Saudis? Or were there others too?*

The chanting and the stream of herded dissenters continued until 11 p.m. when the guerrillas melted away and the bedraggled crowd headed, exhausted and relieved, toward their apartments. Some with gray hair were so tired, they hung on the shoulders of their comrades. Others sprinted away, likely looking for a toilet.

I awakened cramped, having fallen asleep in my chair by the window, and flipped on the TV, expecting a full report. But the newscasters made no mention of the demonstrations, showing only the same video of clerics in photogenic inaction. Esau's funding had not reached the state-controlled news sources yet.

My nights by the window observing the demonstrations continued for a month, until mid-March; and by this time, the state-run news agencies, although they never reported the insurrections, had failed to conceal their existence. The damage was done. The population assumed a new mood of unease. *What is happening among us?* This question hung in the air. *Are we really in revolt against the Ayatollah?* Make-believe rebellion became a rebellion in fact. The café scene changed from one of open, animated discourse to suspicious glances among former friends. Who was listening? Could she, the one in the black *chador*, be with the state?

But for the month, no Esau, just his shadow.

At the ministry, Khadim didn't speak about the civil disturbances either. Nothing even close. And by this time, despite the recent cold shoulder, I had come, in a strange way, to think of him as almost a friend. But now, no eye contact, no tea together unless compelled by the nature of our business and never alone. *Surely, he didn't suspect that I might know the root of the discord. Or did he?*

Then a phone call came in for me on a line at my ministry office. "Meet me tonight in the same café, 7 p.m."

I slammed down the phone. *Was he crazy? Why was he trying to get me caught up in his treachery?* I was frightened and furious at the same time, just like that day in high school so long ago. But I went. *Why did he make me wait again at the cafe?* I knew he did this just to increase my anxiety. I fidgeted in the cold, and rubbed my face to increase circulation.

He arrived at 8. His beard was poorly trimmed, and his belly, not entirely new, but now mature in its breadth. His wrinkles had increased in number and depth. I had expected he would be ebullient about his recent success, but his lips were horizontal and tight and his eyes red. I remembered the sertraline I had seen on his desk at the high school, an antidepressant. Perhaps despondency was still a plague for him? I rejoiced for a moment at his disability, but it was fleeting.

He came alive when he took a seat across from me, sitting up straight with his fists clenched on the table. "Well, Yacoub, what did you think about the demonstrations? Rather effective, don't you think? I hope you're impressed by my degree of control, and I assure you it's even greater than what you've seen so far."

I shifted my weight in the cold metal chair. "Why do you care? Why is any of this important to you? You're a Muslim, or at least you used to be."

"All religions are evil plots. Now we're really going to have some fun."

He pulled out an 8" X 12" manila envelope, relishing the process, and with a flourish, flipped over the photo. "It's a very lovely bomb, is it not?" I had seen one like it in person during my acquisition process. The armament was about six feet long and two feet in width, grey metal with a red, pointed nose and fins on the rear. *No, it was not lovely.* The bomb was intended for placement on a missile or for dropping from a plane. "I'm sure you're familiar with it." I sank into my seat on the metal chair. The bomb would need modification if it was planted in a specific location, but its very appearance neutralized any remaining confidence I might have had.

"You can't explode that thing here in Tehran. It would wipe out the entire city."

"That's exactly what I intend. We'll say the Saudis planted it." *He was getting money from the Saudis.* "What better way is there to start the war that destroys the Middle East with all its so-called religious traditions? The war will spread right away from Tehran to the rest of the Gulf. My dead mother would be proud. And all that pious, holy trash on Failaka will be destroyed, along with the rest of the Gulf states." He knew of Failaka, my father's beloved island in Kuwait Bay, where he had fished as a young man. "But first, I have a request for you to take to Khadim. I want one billion U.S. dollars delivered to my account by June 1, the date the bomb will be exploded if there is no deposit."

Revenge with a dose of greed. While destruction was one aim, the other was financial gain.

"It's up to you how you carry this message, but I'll tell you this: He already knows about me. You'd better make sure I remain safe, or my colleagues will act on June 1 on their own."

Our coffee time was over. The cold sludge in the bottom of my cup was all that was left. Esau rose and slowly walked up the street and turned left at the next corner. *Should I follow him? How was I supposed to keep him safe?* Perhaps I could see his associates, but my indecision rendered that plan defunct. I would have to figure out how to engage Khadim. By the time I reached my flat, I was done, with no strength even to undress. The chair by

179

the window became my bed and my street clothes, my pajamas.

In Psalms 16:8 David had written: "I have set the Lord always before me." The sentence, recalled from my mother's teaching, upset me now. No, it infuriated me. *How could David do this?* It was not possible for any man, certainly not me at this low ebb. I wasn't ready.

I waited two days before confronting Khadim. There was no time for further delay, and the visit was necessary. My collar chafed my neck, and my belt impeded my breathing. *What was the risk of my announcement? Would I go back to Evin, perhaps with new charges brought against me?*

As Khadim's secretary proclaimed my visit over the intercom, there was no choice. I had to go in.

"Sir, I need to speak about a matter of extreme importance to the country." Khadim barely looked up from his computer, left me standing, no tea. Sitting for the explanation had been my source of a small comfort, and now he took that from me too.

"There is news you won't like. I've been informed that a nuclear device will be set off here in the city, if we don't pay a billion dollars. I've seen a photo of the bomb. It's one of mine – ours actually."

Finally, Khadim stopped pecking at his keyboard and whirled around to face me. "I've had it with you. First, I wondered if you knew something about the civil disturbances, and now I'm certain of it." His brown face went red, the veins in his forehead jutting out.

What followed from me was a too-long explanation. Yes, my half-brother (*yes, I had one*) was in on it, he was after me, he had announced himself as the enemy of all religions, and he was serious and dangerous. But I had had some other thoughts on the matter. My two-day hiatus had given me the chance to formulate a plan, which I delivered in double-time, due to my standing position. "We have two months to solve this," I continued. "It's crucial that we find the bomb. How in blazes did he get it without authorities being notified in the first place? There must be accomplices in your, yes your, system." My voice increased in volume. "And I don't care what you think, but this was not my doing. It's yours. And the result will be at your door, not mine." He asked me to sit. I didn't. I just needed to get through this next part. "Even though you are not innocent in all of this, you cannot get involved yourself now. Coming from your position, that'll be too obvious. This is my show now, only mine." Khadim didn't respond, his mouth fell open, and at last he stood with hands on hips.

"Do what you must then," he answered. "Now, get out of here. I'll wait for good news. And if there's none, well, that will be the end of you, too, of both of us actually."

The bomb debacle was now in my hands, and mine alone. Khadim could only make it worse. Somehow, he must be in on it, but I got what I wanted.

Now, I called the shots. Exactly where did the dilemma lie? With me. Both Esau and the bomb were linked chiefly to me; at least that's the way it would come out.

Where was Esau? He was the key, my only clue to the location of the bomb, and he had hidden all his personal information. Was there an excuse for another meeting? I had to wait for his contact. On April 10, he phoned. "Any progress on my money?"

Thus, Esau was lured to our café.

The venue had changed with a new owner, much to my advantage. I was waiting when Esau arrived; and puzzled, he whirled from side to side searching with a vexed expression for the security cameras, which were now concealed in different locations. He saw me, hesitated, another sly glance around for clues, and sat opposite me. There were sweat beads on his upper lip this time, a small victory.

"You have the money?" Was the money more important than his supposed spiritual triumph?

My answer was silence. Keep him guessing.

"What's it going to be anyway – the bomb or the money?"

I wrote my answer on a paper napkin and pushed it in front of him: *Yes, the money is coming.*

With that information, he gave me two weeks, rose and hurried off. The now unfamiliar setting with its new camera system had spooked him.

Suddenly, I found myself in an unlikely role: a neophyte spy tracking a dangerous and experienced menace. Esau had taken a *darbast* cab immediately after rounding the corner, and I grabbed another taxi right behind him, which had just emptied of two foreigners, apparently Americans who smiled at me (Americans were always too friendly). It was like an old movie: *Follow that car!* The two taxis traced their way amid the western Tehran traffic clog: first through Ekbatan Town, ending near Ghazali Cinema Town at the Kouroush Cineplex with its twelve separate theaters and neon architecture. Why here? Esau purchased a ticket to see *Bashu, the Little Stranger*, which tells the story of a child escaping from the terrors of the Iran-Iraq war. *Did he know I followed?* OK, so maybe he wanted to see a tearjerker about an awful war, just a warm up to what he intended. Another ticket for me and then I sat in a strategic seat five rows behind Esau, my hands prayerfully folded in front of me, covering my face.

Esau hooked his thumbs in his belt and tilted his head against the headrest. Was he sleeping? After thirty minutes, a woman with a head covering took the seat by him, ignoring other available seating, not a suitable or typical choice for an Iranian female. They didn't make eye contact. *How strange!*

After another thirty minutes, and still without a glance between them, he handed her a folded sheet of paper. She got up from her seat and headed for the exit door in the rear of the theater. Should I stay with Esau or follow her? There was no rational basis for the choice, but I followed her.

In the now dark, emptying streets, there were no cabs in sight and little traffic, which made this simpler for me. After several blocks she entered one of the few late-night clubs in Tehran, usually prohibited for women. Two five thousand rial notes to the doorman secured my entry. She immediately proceeded to the back corner of the establishment where several unused water pipes for smoking remained, nodded to the owner, and assumed the position of an experienced smoker, sucking air into the water pipe to freshen the coals. The acrid smoke in the room nearly made me cough. My eyes burned. Another woman soon joined her. After sharing the same apparatus for several minutes, the new woman took the paper, and left. What was I following the paper or the person? I elected for the paper.

Here I was again following a woman on the already darkened streets – a practice which might brand me as a mark for the police. Three blocks later at the edge of the cinema district, she rapped five times on the metal door of a brick building, perhaps a warehouse. After the door opened, a man's hand took the paper and shut the door. For whatever it was worth, I now had the address of the warehouse, so I resumed following the woman, who continued for several blocks finally entering an apartment building on Laheh Boulevard. Shortly after that, the light blinked on in a third floor flat. I stayed and watched from a shadowed doorway, and awhile later, Esau and the first woman from the movie theater entered the same building. Did Esau have two accomplices, two wives? What an enterprising man, and how well he had adapted to Islam, the religion he said he had rejected.

I couldn't resist. I returned to the apartment building at 6 the next morning, more curious than ever. The sun peeked around the buildings, shadows forming on the pavement below. The garbage trucks rounded the corner, their stench assaulting my senses. Then, more than the odor, I was struck by the appearance of the same two women emerging from the building. This time they were unmistakably dressed as members of the women's *Basij*, the paramilitary group which was a civilian subsidiary of the Revolutionary Guards. Esau had astonished me again. *How had he accomplished this level of engagement in the Iranian government, culture, and religion in such a short time, and all for a reprehensible purpose? And he didn't believe in any of the three: Sunni, Shia, or Christian!*

I now possessed two pieces of new information: the warehouse site, surely the location of the bomb, and Esau's address. How to use the data? I had to think it through. One thing was sure: I couldn't take it to Khadim. My trust account there was closed, at least for now. If I took what I knew up the line, at some point, I'd hit the giant obstacle, the big trap – the person in the government who was in on it, the one who had procured the bomb in the first place. That was the only way Esau could have gotten hold of it. And the Basij were certainly involved. No, I had to solve it with my own means.

I remembered a Shia friend from Evin, a former cleric, one who had threatened to reveal the thefts of the Ayatollah and his colleagues. Hamid was released by now, no longer allowed to ply his trade of organized religion. Finding him was no problem, as he couldn't separate himself from his former mosque, the Soltani Mosque in the Grand Bazaar area. I took a taxi and found him in the entry courtyard, sitting and crying, head bowed.

I walked across the quadrangle in front of the two blue, white, and yellow spires, from which the muezzins called the faithful to prayer, the cleaners sweeping the dust between them with straw brooms, worshippers awaiting the next call, all ignoring the penitent, black-bearded, wailing imam. He no longer existed to them.

"Hamid, make yourself erect," I spoke forcefully. "We must rescue your country."

"You, a Jesus-worshipper, can do nothing here." His head fell again into his cloak.

"What we believe doesn't matter now. There is a bomb that will be ignited in Tehran. I need your help." The bomb was the issue, forget the two billion dollars.

"An explosion is better than apostasy; the bigger the bomb, the better." Hamid was morose, defeated. *How much time did he spend here weeping? I did not know.*

Slowly and carefully, I quietly explained the full story to Hamid. He had no one of importance, no one who would listen, to tell, so I felt assured of his silence.

Finally, the response of the patriot, the true believer in Islam came to the fore. "Here's what we must do. I have friends, who are not accomplices of the Ayatollah. They will assist. We must get rid of this Esau, the one who takes two women, as if he has the same rights as a true Muslim. He's a deceiver." Finally, a compatriot and possibly, a way.

###

Hamid said Esau must be the first target, and I agreed. Strong arms were required. Hamid supplied them, and the scene required my pleasurable vigilance.

Two nights later at 2 a.m., outside the apartment on Laheh, four of us, three giants supplied by Hamid and myself, encamped on the street, waiting for Esau to enter the building. Esau and his two chador-clothed wives arrived and the apartment light went on. We sounded like an army going up the creaky stairs to the third floor. *Surely they heard us.* "A gas leak has been reported in the building. We need to check your apartment." An attempt at easy access.

"We don't have gas."

With that, the largest of my giant accomplices hurled his frame against the door, which crumpled open at the latch, the metal wrested from the wood. There was no bolt. Even the sturdy Esau was dwarfed and quickly brought under control. The two women, however, still draped in black, were another matter. Wailing and shrieking, they attacked with clenched fists and a vase within reach. A gash over my left eye poured blood onto my white shirt collar. These two women did not practice the Western custom of using deodorant and taking frequent showers, and their pungency just added to the assault. But my giants were up to the task. Pretty quickly, the women were tied, gagged, and pushed to the floor. Esau was tied up with thick, white rope and gagged with a torn fragment of a chador. Giant Number One took out his cell and called our pick-up car. At the sidewalk I saw the black Suburban, which rekindled the memory of my ride to Evin, and now we pushed Esau into the same. I hurt all over thinking of the long ride before us.

The night was still dark when we passed through the holy city of Qom, then on to the south. We had ten more hours to go. By late afternoon we arrived at Bandar Abbas, where I had shipping connections because of my earlier job in getting the materials for the bombs. The Sunni city with its men dressed in robes and head coverings looked more like an Arab metropolis than Tehran. Heading toward the docks for smaller boats, we encountered two white and green patrolling police cars, lights blinking, sirens wailing. I wondered aloud if they would want to search what was behind our darkened windows, and Esau squirmed in his tethers, trying to place his blindfolded face against the window. Too late for him – the police were chasing others.

My friend who piloted the thirty-meter sloop *Dove* greeted us at the pier, and he dumped our wriggling cargo into his hold so fast that we didn't even confer. Esau kicked the side of the craft until he was secured to the bunk. Giant Number One accompanied the *Dove* on the ten-hour voyage across the Strait of Hormuz to Ras Al Khaimah, and we waited in the Suburban for our large colleague to return. The two remaining giants ate pretzels and smoked Special Oshno cigarettes. I cracked the window.

When the *Dove* returned the next day, Giant Number One confirmed the transfer. All of Esau's travel and identity documents had been taken and were handed to me. So much for that part of the problem.

When I arrived back in Tehran, I used my ministry computer connections to remove all evidence of his residency and even his existence in Iran, including his driver's license, auto ownership record, banking and housing information. Esau had never lived in Iran. The fate of his two wives? No bother for now.

That one-billion-dollar portion of the problem was fixed, but there was one more issue. The bomb itself. *How many times would this problem I created return to persecute me?*

CHAPTER 13

THE BOMB

This job was too big for me, even with the three giants. If we recovered the weapon, what would we do with it? I needed Khadim's resources, but I'd already excluded him from the process, regrettable but necessary.

I needed help from a faction totally outside the political/economic/religious conglomerate I was in. There could be no possibility of any unexpected connections. They had to have access to a location to dispose of the weapon too.

An odd solution came to me. I would ask my friends at the Brethren Evangelical Church to meet with me. I had encountered two of their leaders during my confinement at Evin. After three taxi rides around the city and several furtive walks to make sure I wasn't being followed, I entered their little gray brick chapel on Fatimah Street. If I was followed, it might be the end for them too. The brethren had once told me about their sister church in Rasht near the Anzali Port to the north on the Caspian Sea. My desperate thinking led me to consider the sea as a safe place to ditch the bomb.

Six of us gathered in the prayer room, which was barren of

any ornamentation except the straight-backed wooden chairs. They assumed it was serious or I wouldn't have come to them. No smiles among us. Surely, I was there for trouble. "Brothers, I must tell you of a dire threat among us." Now, definitely no smiles, hands folded, rigid necks. I gave few details; as too much information would expose my own role. The fact that there was a nuclear weapon set to explode in our midst was sufficient.

"Why us?"

"You're the only ones I can trust. I know you have no connections whatsoever to the government. You also have access to the only place I can think of to dispose of the bomb, through your colleagues up on the Caspian, where we could just dump it in the water." No green solution here. "My contacts in the ministry can't be trusted. I don't know where the bomb came from and I don't know where it could end up." Only partial truths. None of the six responded.

Only then did I explain the remainder of my plan, and they excused me to the outer room while they discussed and prayed. Loud voices, some angry, emanated from their privacy. Thirty minutes elapsed, then forty-five.

At 6 p.m., they answered, "Yes, we'll do it."

At 2 a.m. two days later, ten unlikely looking, balding middle-aged men and a six-meter red panel truck with no identification stopped in front of the warehouse. We exited the vehicle, and I rapped on the metal door five times, the same signal I had heard before. As the door opened, all of us swept in and overcame the two supposed bomb-sitters, who bit two of the men and spat on the rest of us. The place smelled like they were lacking a working toilet. We bound the two with ropes and gagged them with rags we had brought. Silence intervened as we began our search for the bomb. We ran from room to room, all three floors, finding nothing but the smell of excrement and cigarettes on the lower floor and dust on the upper levels. Failure overcame me, my shoulders drooped, and I couldn't speak. Such a carefully laid plan and now no result. The warehouse had been just a decoy all the time. The brethren were too kind to speak, but we were all discouraged. A few of them didn't make eye contact. Surely they were done with any more plans from me.

What to do with our bound captives, looking up at us with wide eyes, perhaps expecting death at our hands? Apologize? We could torture them to learn about the bomb, but none of us had the cruelty required. Brother Andrew untied the guards. "We're very sorry for your trouble," he told them. They scrambled for the door, and at the street one ran left and the other right. Had the bomb ever been there in the first place? I thanked the men for trying to help me, and we discussed what to do next.

And so it was that we ended up back at the apartment of Esau's two wives. "Where have you taken our husband?" they demanded. The brethren stuck with me, but they were less confident with my scheme now.

"Where's the bomb?" I countered. *We had to know. Now.*

Upon being informed that Esau was somewhere on the other

side of the Gulf, headed in a direction unknown to me, perhaps trapped in the desert, both women sobbed and wailed. I was completely unprepared for their emotional response. Somehow I had thought their relationship was based on political convenience. My skewed opinion was that Esau was incapable of close relationships. Apparently I was wrong about this too.

"You must help us get to him. Then, we'll tell you where your silly bomb is," they answered together. The brethren remained speechless, slack-jawed that I had involved them in what had turned into such a taut and risky venture, and more so, an invasion of Esau's family. I realized that this had gone to a new level now. I turned and thanked my friends again for helping me. We would not get any further today. They excused themselves, hands in pockets, heads down. I could not call on them again. What a crazy situation I had entangled these faithful, peaceful men in. I was more ashamed now than at any other any point in the entire mess.

The women went to their bedrooms where they put on their chadors, and the three of us sat down facing each other on the thin-cushioned chairs. They were no longer crying but leaned forward to hear my non-existent solution.

"There's nothing I can do. The only connection I have is Kuwait. Maybe I could get you to Kuwait, but about your husband…" On the mantle I saw a picture of an older Caucasian woman. Esau's mother?

"Well, no husband for us, no bomb for you. The bomb is under the control of our people. When we get our husband, we'll tell you where it is," they replied.

Was this the best deal I could make? Women supposedly had no power in the Persian government, or did they have some after all? Clearly these two women had some clout after all, my only shred of hope. As unlikely as it seemed, Esau now prevented the very destruction he had meant to produce, and I could only continue to persist in my uncertainty. I still had no idea how this drama would unfold.

I did have to report to Khadim. A group was meeting in his office. When I cracked open the door, he saw me and waved out the flotilla of suits and ties, all apparently business types. They stopped talking and looked at each other, as if to ask *why*.

He motioned me in but gave no invitation to sit.

"Good news, we don't have to come up with the money" Of course, the money would not have been a problem. "And the bomb is secure." *Close to a lie.*

"Where is it?"

"I don't know but I'm sure it's safe." *Definitely a lie.* Its safety was predicated on the word of the two women, who expected me to get them back to their husband. The only reason it had not been detonated was because they had somehow prevented that. This had become so complicated. I had backed myself into a corner, and there were no further choices open to me. I was not sure what to do next.

Khadim jumped up from his chair, which crashed against the wall behind him, and smashed the screen of his computer with a tea glass. And he was a slave to his computer. "Get out of here. We never had this conversation. I have no knowledge of any of this. This never happened."

Khadim's last statement raised a question in my mind I had not considered. *Why didn't he know the bomb was missing, even before I knew? Why wouldn't he tell me the truth?*

For the remainder of my "imprisonment," I floundered in this neverland: a bomb of my making was out there, somewhere in hiding, perhaps possessed by those more dangerous than even Esau. My relationship with Khadim was done – there was no trust between us. At least he couldn't send me back to Evin. For him to do so would be to raise the question: Why?

My stay in this setting and current mindset continued until early 2021, the time of my release. I watched those around me grow in their faith. I knew they had advanced because I saw their courage increase in the face of state vigilance. Why did I hear no more about the bomb? Was it all an empty threat? I had no idea what the bomb owners' objective really was now.

Iran had the bomb, but other countries still speculated about their possession of it. The country had weathered the bond crisis in remarkable fashion. I could not avoid thinking: *These were both my doing.* My pride was stained with regret. I still couldn't articulate what I wanted out of all this.

The gospel of Jesus spread like water, seeping into any crevice. The government was at a loss as to how to handle its advance. To even admit its success and publicly attack it, would be defeat for them, so quiet reigned. Critical mass had been reached, and the government chose to be silent about what it could not control.

With all I had done, I was still immensely relieved to get out of Iran and go home. Being thrust back to little Kuwait and whatever confusion I would encounter there was much better than living under the constant stress of my watchful keepers in Tehran.

CHAPTER 14

FACING MY FEARS

As I emerged from the Kuwait airport terminal, the dry, cool winter adorned by the blinding sun greeted me. The dust persisted. I had forgotten: No place on earth has more dust than Kuwait.

Following the Trump debacle in the first years of his presidency, the United States had calmed somewhat, and there were renewed thoughts of stability for the Middle East, a hope that had no basis in reality.

My father, whom I had not expected to make the airport trip, was there to greet me. He was 83 now, and still did not require help beyond his cane. He was dressed in the winter dark gray dishdasha and red-and-white-checkered keffiyeh head covering. As we embraced, I felt how prominent his ribs had become. The skin on his hands and wrists was thin, and easy bruising was evident.

Hibah accompanied him. She maintained her hair covering with a bright yellow scarf, just enough to pass the propriety test for a conservative Arab female. She was now a mature young woman, still unmarried and expanding her now-competitive law practice.

Binyamin was there too, now eighteen, already sporting a thick beard.

The ride home, beyond their pointing out all the building projects, was quiet. Ugly construction crane dragons swung in arcs all over the city. The building of large physical structures abounded in Kuwait. As a result of the construction contests among Gulf countries, the towering buildings, often with numerous vacancies, were all too common. Appearance counted for more than substance.

We arrived back at our old home in Ahmadi, oil wells within earshot nearby pumping away, raping the already pummeled earth. As soon as we were inside our gate, the white walls shielded us from the repulsive rhythm. My father and Hibah were kind enough not to make many inquiries about my long sojourn in Tehran, but Binyamin wanted every detail, and I acquiesced. "Little brother, there's much to tell." And for two hours I went on.

But I had many questions which I did not ask. What would my status be in Kuwait now? *How strange that this was my first thought.* Did people know the circumstances, cause, and course of my detention? As always, I inflated the importance of my own position in my mind. In point of fact, other than by my family, I had been little missed. I would have to tell the story of my time in Iran if it was to be repeated. But certainly not all of it – not the torture and not my own betrayal. *And where was the bomb? In Kuwait?* Yes, I had gotten rid of Esau by exporting him by force out of Iran. But now, in Kuwait, what was he up to? Perhaps he was still in possession of that bomb? I had failed to deal with his presence in Kuwait.

How had Kuwait weathered the bond crisis? The restructuring of debt among Kuwaiti entrepreneurs had taken place all too quickly and without adequate financial planning, but the inherent wealth of the country and the money in the ground were still considered sufficient by all. "The Manakh financial crisis of the early 80s is long forgotten, and even the recent bond disaster is a distant memory," my father recalled. "The next such event will be a surprise, too." He reminded me how he had escaped the Manakh disaster through the wisdom of my mother. He always reminded me of her. "She had no training in finance, but she knew the Manakh would collapse before anyone else."

Liberal elements in the city competed with extreme conservative groups to the extent that there was nothing else in the news. The *Kuwait Times* editorial of February 26, 2021, Kuwait Liberation Day, read, "As we celebrate our liberation from Iraq in 1991, we are now our own enemy. Two extreme factions, both counter to the Kuwaiti ideal of the middle ground, conflict with each other with no logical basis for meaningful resolution. Neither side cares about the future of our nation state. The question extant is whether the opposing factions will allow the peace of Kuwait to persist as it has in our long history. With ongoing events, it seems not. The religious extremists have always shown violent tendencies, but now the same is true of the liberal elements. Where will this end?"

A subtext to this wrangling was the unfolding work of the gospel among Kuwaitis. My father and I sat in the leather-chaired study after dinner and Hibah soon joined us. Binyamin entered, eating a peanut butter sandwich. He had achieved adult status, free to listen to all the trouble. The furniture and old pictures were still the same. A photo of my great-grandfather sat on a table. Everything was old, the furniture the same as from my childhood, except for the sixty-five-inch skinny TV, whose clarity amazed me. Hibah invited Divina in with us as well. Divina had assumed the role of the senior woman of the family, formerly played by my mother, Rabea. Together, they told me their stories, and brought me up-to-date on all that had occurred during my detention.

My father leaned forward in his leather chair. "Thanks to God, the government has become even more dysfunctional. The liberal-extremist conflict has consumed all their resources, and the state expends their resources there, mainly going after the extremists. U.S. interference has only made this worse." Another Trump residual. "The secret police infiltrates both sides, imagining they're protecting the country. They know Christians aren't a safety risk, and it's deemed in the interest of the government not to even mention that there are increasing numbers of Kuwaiti Christians."

"How many are there?" The greater the number, the higher the vulnerability.

"We avoid numerical estimates. We don't want numbers repeated. But the number has exploded. The growth has occurred mainly by the usual means: one telling another. There have been dreams, but not many."

"How do you worship?

My father cleared his throat and launched into the details. Perhaps he wanted me to ask. "There are several forms, and nothing is standardized. Some still go to the mosque. We've abandoned that. I couldn't tolerate the sense of compromise I had in my heart any longer. Some just stay in their own homes for worship." He reached over to the table and picked up a map. "Most of us meet in house churches, small with just a few families. There are other so-called house churches, but these are really large halls that have been secured for worship. As many as fifty attend. The secret service shuns them. To acknowledge them would create a third threat in the news. Probably they're watching from a distance. Ours is right here." He pointed out the location.

Hibah said proudly, "Your father leads the one he's showing you."

Now I was really concerned, "But the risk?" For years now, my main concern had been risk.

"I'm 83 years old. God can have me any time he wants. What's the danger?"

"What does the service look like?"

"Tomorrow you'll see.

Hibah told me of her work. "It's been difficult with the women. They're still subject in every way to their husbands, even though they're Christian. We're talking with women from all walks. Many don't know how to respond, and they aren't accustomed to making their own decisions. It seems easier for the more educated, but even there…" Her words were optimistic, but she cast her eyes downward periodically, and didn't smile. Unlike me, she knew her role.

"Then how do these women come to Jesus?" I bent forward and took a date from the platter with my fingers. Hibah handed me a napkin. She didn't want her carpet sullied by her newly arrived brother.

"With all the gender problems, they still come. It's a miracle. The men who are converted bring their women along. That's what happens most often. Whether you call that conversion or not, who knows? God knows." Hibah nodded to Divina, "The maids are a secret weapon. They talk with the women. They answer questions the women ask when they're at home without the men around." This was Divina's work. "Divina has taught the ex-patriot maids how to go about presenting the gospel in the home in which they work." Divina glanced down, without acknowledging the praise. I envied the godly humility of both women.

The next morning was Friday, and we went to the hall my father had rented for the service. I was skittish, my default state. "The Lord is my light and my salvation; whom shall I fear?" (Psalm 27:1). The psalms of my dead mother mocked me again.

The empty hall was in a quiet neighborhood in Qurtoba off Abu Ayyub Al-Ansari Street. There was no specific parking area, so those attending scattered their vehicles throughout the neighborhood. This way the meeting was not so obvious.

The worshippers filed quietly into the large, bare room with folding chairs already set up. An elevated table was placed in the front on a makeshift stage. The room was unheated and cold in the midwinter morning. The men and women sat together with no evidence of segregation. Binyamin sat next to a young girl I didn't recognize. Hibah later told me my father required this seating arrangement in order to dispel any evidence of gender inequality before God. Most of the women were still covered.

I counted fifty-six congregants.

My father stood silently at the front by the table for a full two minutes while the congregation bowed their heads. I waited uncomfortably for something to happen. Then, my father looked to Mohammed on his right near the front. For forty years Mohammed had been the muezzin of the area mosque. For forty years he had called the people to prayer five times daily. But the grizzled, shrunken old man had dreamed a dream. Now he called the church of Jesus to prayer. Mohammed rose. His voice was still deep and rich, and he gave melody to a psalm by the rhythm of his recitation, "Shout for joy to God, all the earth; sing the glory of his name; give to him glorious praise! Say to God, 'How awesome are your deeds! So great is your power that your enemies come cringing to you. All the earth worships you and sings praises to you; they sing praises to your name'" (Psalm 66:1-4). I shivered, chilled in the cool air.

The hymn singing in the church was from the Psalms. Two traditional Kuwaiti musicians accompanied the congregation with the ten string oud and small drums. As there was much modern Arabic Christian music available, I asked my father about this choice later. "I know about that music, but I want the Kuwaiti church to develop its own worship from the very beginning. Psalms are a good beginning."

In the middle of the service my father stood and prayed for the needs of the church: for the rental of the building, those who were sick, and the financial needs of several. He expressed thanks to God for His protection from persecution. After closing the prayer in the name of Jesus, he asked the flock to place their financial gifts in the small box at the door as they departed later.

To my shock, Hibah rose from her seat and began to sing. I had never heard her before. She sang without accompaniment, and her voice was high, sweet and clear. The song was that of Moses and Miriam, "I will sing to the Lord, for he has triumphed gloriously; the horse and his rider he has thrown into the sea. The Lord is my strength and my song... this is my God, and I will praise him, my father's God, and I will exalt him" (Exodus 15:1-2). For a moment I saw the shadow of my mother.

My father propped himself on his cane and stood at the table. I was surprised at his choice of a text too. I thought it quite difficult. It was Galatians 5:1-14. He preached in the circular manner long established in the Middle East, known to both Arab and Jew and all Semitic peoples, often seen in the Scriptures, as it was in this passage. There was none of the three-point syllogism method here that was typical in Western churches. His method was faithful to Paul's. The beginning and end of the passage emphasized our freedom only in Christ. "For freedom Christ has set us free

(Galatians 5:1a)."

The middle of the passage presented a difficult concept, that the Old Testament Law, or Sharia law, could never make us free but only enslave us. My father said, "We are slaves if we live only by the Law. No law can make us right with God. The Law does not work for our salvation because we cannot fully obey it. If we try to obey a small part of the Law, like circumcision, the rest of the Law is still there to convict us. We still have the desires of our flesh. Paul says the only way to obey the whole Law is to cut off all of our desires, not just the foreskin, as he says in Galatians 5:12, 'I wish those who unsettle you would emasculate themselves.' By this Paul meant that the only way to obey the whole Law was to amputate the entire organ, not just a part of it. Only then, by removing the entire source of desires could the Law be obeyed." The passage concluded with: "For you were called to freedom, brothers (Galatians 5:13a)." My father completed the circle of the passage, "For the whole law is fulfilled in one word: 'You shall love your neighbor as yourself'" (Galatians 5:14).

I thought the passage was too much for most to absorb, but to my surprise the people were rapt in their attention, nodding in agreement. I had not noticed Thawab in the congregation, but at my father's direction he arose, lifted his arms and said, "May the God of hope fill you with all joy and peace in believing, so that by the power of the Holy Spirit you may abound in hope" (Romans 15:13). With that benediction the congregation rose and filed out of the building. Greetings and conversations, men and women together, took place on the grounds for about thirty minutes.

The whole experience was too much for me. I couldn't believe what had gone on in my absence. *God had bypassed me! Would my Persian bomb sins follow me? Did I cause the bomb to end up in Kuwait? And what's more, with the burgeoning churches, Esau had a real target. What if the bomb really was in Kuwait?* I pictured the explosion at my father's church.

How could I fail to see the Lord's hand? What was the grand plan? Was I a part of it? Unlike God, I couldn't see the end from the beginning. I was finally beginning to see my limitations. *How could I have been so blind?*

Despite the progress of the gospel in Kuwait, there were threats. Most of these originated in quarters that were isolated and without the means to cause difficulty. But one of the threats surprised and frightened me. I shouldn't have been surprised, as it only confirmed my fears. That threat was my half-brother, Esau... again.

CHAPTER 15

"ESAU WILL BE STUBBLE"

I had hoped to rid my family and myself of Esau, leaving him on that sad little stretch of land across from Bandar Abbas. But he was not so easily eliminated. "You need to know what's happening with your brother, your half-brother," said my father. He sat in his well-padded chair. "His ISIS colleagues found him on that strand of land and got him to Qatar. And then here to Kuwait." *So my efforts had failed miserably, and Esau had not been held there in Qatar as planned.* I suspected there was still a lot my father hadn't told me. From his grim countenance, it was clear the Esau situation had only worsened. Esau had become an agent of extreme Islam in Kuwait, at least that was my father's analysis. Of course, there was more, more on the personal side.

"Dr. Allison, Esau's mother, chose the name *Esau* purposefully. She was a student of history, and the significance of the name was not lost on her. She resented the circumstances of our affair, even though she dictated the course of events. It was my fault too, but she begrudged my returning to the wealth of Kuwait and leaving her with the responsibility. I paid for my departure many times over, at least in dinars."

My father was more forthcoming now than when I was a teenager, but the Esau story always depressed him. He sank into the wrinkles in his neck. "Before Esau's mother died, she insisted that I only came back to Kuwait to be rich, but I think the crowning irritation was the fact that I became a Christian. She learned about my conversion when she came to Kuwait on a sabbatical for an archeological dig many years ago – that geological attack of hers on Failika. For her, my conversion was an affront to her sensibilities, impossible for her to integrate into her image of me. She thought it was all fake. I tried to speak with her when she was here, in order to set things straight, but I failed."

"I don't get it," I replied. "I thought I understood it when I was in school. Esau was after me while I was in Iran, but I still don't grasp why Esau's so against us. I understand all you've said, but it doesn't seem sufficient to explain the extreme passion behind his attacks."

"His mother came to despise me. That's what she said. Eventually she wouldn't even talk to me. I know much of this was my sin." I could see he was tired and only with urging did the story leak out. "I know it doesn't make sense. The fact is that she resented me, even though, in my view, she took advantage of me. She blackmailed me and threatened to tell Rabea. She wrote me that she had been diagnosed with breast cancer. It had spread. She knew she was going to die, and I was to blame. She didn't write that exactly, but that was her message. I was the ruin of her life."

"But what about Esau?"

"He came to Kuwait shortly after her death. That's what ignited his fire. That's when he came to your school as headmaster. He was more definite with me than he was with you. He blamed me for the condition in which his mother died. He said I was responsible for her emotional and physical decline by my neglect." The old man had to gather his thoughts before continuing, preventing the flow of tears. "I didn't deny this. I was responsible. I deserted her with a failing marriage. The end of her marriage left her with insufficient resources. Of course, I paid for Esau's education at Stanford, but I gave nothing of myself to either of them. All that I did not do got magnified over the years. That's the way it's been since he first arrived here. He was gone for a time, but now he's back. And it's worse, much worse."

"How so?" I didn't fill in the details I knew about Esau's absence from Kuwait. I should have known he'd make it back to Kuwait from Ras Al-Khaimah. I really didn't want my father to carry on like this, but I honored his apparent need.

"I know you're well-acquainted with the name of your half-brother. There's a verse in the book of Obadiah that says, 'The house of Jacob shall be a fire, and the house of Joseph a flame, and the house of Esau stubble; they shall burn them and consume them, and there shall be no survivor for the house of Esau, for the Lord has spoken' (Obadiah 1:18). The stage had been set from the beginning. Esau and his mother adopted this old conflict and made it their mission in life." My father looked down, as if he was the one responsible. *In point of fact, I thought I was the guilty one.* "I wouldn't give his mother credit for a prophecy," my father continued, "but Esau's here and he's already demonstrated the works of his hand. He also understand the words in the Bible and he knows it's his death struggle. For some reason, that does not deter him."

"So it's worse." I kept learning more than I wanted to know.

"He's brought devastation wherever he's been. He set the Al Ahli Bank on its ear. He came in there as a midlevel executive and cleverly managed to turn the bank executives against one another. He instigated arguments among them and used the fights to win advantage. He was hospitalized back in the United States – shock treatments for depression." *I should have guessed.* "Then, he came back to the Al-Bader Trading Company and got in with their advanced computer system. Somehow he's maintained ties with the Al-Ahli Bank, even with all the trouble he caused there. He's still at the top after freezing out better, kinder men." I saw my father wanted to be alone, but Hibah entered the room with tea and crackers. She looked distressed at our father's confessions, but he had to continue.

"His personal life is the same – four wives in ten years, still married to two, and living with a fifth woman, with six children. None of his personal life affects us, but he's carrying out his mission against the fledgling church."

"By what means?" The discussion was taking far too long for my taste. I just wanted simple answers, and I wanted to stop punishing our father by his endless telling. *Just a solution, please. What was Esau doing? How could we stop him?*

"It's said he's joined ISIL and that he's organizing a cell here in

Kuwait." I knew from Esau's comments to me in Iran that he was actually the enemy of any religion, but he was adept at playing all sides just the same. "We still don't know if that's true. And it seems contradictory, but he probably has connections in Iran. And why in the world with the Shia?" *I knew that to be fact.* "Of course, he's a computer expert. Our computer traffic in regard to the church has undoubtedly been invaded. Like a hungry lion he goes from one threat to another. He has no discipline, even toward his own aims." The old photos around our living room formed a variegated backdrop of the past, racing camels from my grandfather's time, a pearl-diving dhow slogging through a windswept sea. "He jumps from one job to another. He singles out various converts, particularly new converts, and tries to frighten them. He sees me as his main enemy. His primary weapon right now is the computer. He's brilliant. He's unstable, with highs and lows like you wouldn't believe. And if it's true, the ISIL connection indicates there may be physical violence in the offing. Binyamin is our only, our best, computer defense."

Papa hadn't touched the tea and crackers. Hibah told me later that Papa's appetite had waned.

"I have to see him again. I want to find out what we're dealing with. I was barely out of my childhood when we first met." Again, I omitted the Iranian business I had with Esau. "After all, he's my brother. I'll phone him."

My father shook his head, as if to say, it won't help.

Two days passed before I summoned the courage to call.

213

"Good morning. This is Yusef Al-Tamimi. I just returned to Kuwait. Perhaps we could meet soon."

"I've been expecting your call. Come to my home on Gulf Road tonight at seven." His voice was even, showing no emotion.

I pulled up at the home as directed; the iron gate was closed. The location by the sea and the palatial size of the home indicated he had done well financially. But the source? How had he recovered so quickly? Corinthian-style columns, out of place in Kuwait, adorned the front of the three-story house. The sleepy Pakistani attendant, wearing a wrinkled white dishdasha, came out of the gatehouse, inquired about my purpose, opened the gate, and I pulled into the driveway circle. There were two small, dark-skinned children playing by the pool, an Indian woman in a sari watching over them. I was ushered into the living room by a male Indian servant. The stairs and floor were marble, and the French antique furniture was heavy and painful to sit upon.

After twenty minutes Esau came downstairs and into the room dressed like a Kuwaiti with a grey winter dishdasha and bare feet. He was now quite obese and had deep facial folds. I was shaken how much he had aged, even since our earlier encounter. My mind went back again to the pills on his principal desk, the sertraline. Did he still take the antidepressant? And then there had been the shock treatments. The servant brought tea.

How odd that I, as a Kuwaiti, wore a woolen sport coat.

"I didn't think you'd come. Look, I'll be clear. Nothing has changed. I have no respect for your family, and I still I want to

214

finish Christianity in Kuwait. That's the main reason I'm here. By any means, and I mean any means, I intend to bring this about. I'm sure you remember how I made your school year difficult. What do think happened to your converted friends in Iran? Do you think it just occurred, an accident? No, definitely not. There's going to be more of the same, but much worse."

"Hasn't your anger worn itself out?" For a brief moment, I saw the sadness of the man. The thought came to me: *He's looking forward to his next prey. He never looks me in the eye.*

"You've talked with your father, our father. It's because of you I have no birthright."

"Mr. Allison, despite what you've said, I have no animosity toward you. The high school thing has worn off. It was long ago." Here in Kuwait I still felt compelled to address him as Mr. "Is there any sort of settlement you're looking for? You must know I had to get you out of Iran. There was no choice there." I was not hopeful but I had to try.

"I'm here for my mother. I can't bring her back, but I can come after you and your father. I'll finish you and all the Christians in Kuwait before you get started on your next thing. I can't stand the sight of you. The fact I may resemble you, when I look in the mirror, is more than I can stand. The truth is that you will be responsible for the future. You can just imagine what I have waiting for you, a remnant of your work in Iran."

"From what I've observed the Lord is doing here in Kuwait, the result, I think, will not be in your favor." I said this with more vigor than I really possessed. *Why was the Lord putting me the midst of all this?*

The evening was quickly concluded. The tea untouched. "Save me, O God! For the waters have come up to my neck. I sink in the deep mire, where there is no foothold." Psalm 69:1-2 occupied my thoughts. Could he really engulf us? I feared my half-brother.

The *Kuwait Times* the next day demonstrated Esau's influence. Was it a coincidence that this new attack appeared just after my visit? The headline read, "Al Ahli Bank Calls in All Loans to Christians." The text of the article continued, "In an unprecedented move, the Al Ahli Bank, by the direction of its administrative staff, has notified Christians that their loans are immediately called for full payment. This action was alarming to the ministers of the State of Kuwait, and the Finance Minister has taken up inquiry into the matter. According to unnamed sources, their action will be reported soon. The names of those from whom payment is demanded includes a number of prominent Kuwaiti families who are identified as Christians in the text of the Al Ahli Bank release. The *Times* has elected not to publish the list of Kuwaitis who are identified as Christians without further information."

We knew Esau still had connections with the bank, but he turned out to be more influential than we suspected. We soon learned he had been installed on their board of directors. Now there was no question about the origin of the bank action.

To no one's surprise the investigation of the Ministry of Finance was swift, cursory, and without effect. They announced that the ministry had evaluated the action from a financial standpoint and conferred with the Justice Ministry to determine its legality. The finding of the two ministries was that the bank's action had been completely within their right as a private financial institution.

The Al Ahli Bank action took the small Kuwaiti Christian community by surprise. In order to save those who couldn't pay off the loans, those who were able paid the debts for them. The selfless response of those who gave out of their own funds actually had the effect of bringing the Kuwaiti Christians closer together. In this respect the Al Ahli Bank action had the exact opposite result from what Esau intended. In addition, many Kuwaiti Christians suddenly became debt-free and more trusting in their brethren than ever before.

Those close to the situation confirmed that Esau Allison was responsible for the bank's course. In the absence of the *Times* reporting the names, the list of the Christians appeared on the bank's website, thus exposing them. But most alarming was the fact that the bank even knew the names of the Kuwaitis who were Christians. How had this information become available? *Why had such a list even been made?* The financial aspects were important, but the real risk was the fact that Islamist elements in the community might feel compelled to act violently on that information.

When I saw that the names were listed, I knew instantly that the information had been obtained by invasion of personal e-mail accounts. The one who had the greatest access to these accounts was Esau Allison.

Three days later the newspaper reported that a Kuwaiti family, a man and his wife and their three children, had been run off the road and killed by an unknown assailant in a gray Ford F-250 truck. There were few other details in the report, but those in the Christian community knew they were fellow believers: Their names had been listed on the Al Ahli Bank site. A week later ISIL claimed credit for the killings, and concern among Kuwaiti Christians rose to a new level. Our potential threats were now physical in addition to financial.

My father took the responsibility on his own shoulders. He rose in church the next Friday. He was stooped in his posture. "My loved ones, I want you to be cautious and vigilant. There are wolves tracking us. We've lost a brother, sister, and their children."

Due to the new indications that ISIL was active in Kuwait, the U.S. Embassy in Kuwait raised the alarm with their State Department, and an additional detachment of Marines was sent to the embassy. This action failed to encourage the Kuwaiti citizenry, as the insertion of various levels of U.S. intervention into other areas of ISIL activity, such as Iraq, Syria, Libya, and Tunisia, had achieved little or nothing and likely made their situations worse. The thinking among most Middle East observers was that ISIL actually benefitted from American attempts at countering their actions. Even though ISIL had lost considerable territory, gone were Mosul and Raqqa, they were now a mobile force.

On the morning of June 6, 2021, ISIL combatants, identified by observers because of their black flag, armed with .50 caliber automatic weapons, mounted on three black Toyota Tacoma pickups, attacked the small Kuwaiti military outpost at Wafra near the Saudi border. Small arms fire continued for two hours. The Kuwaiti detachment had sufficient weaponry to stave off the attack, and the vehicles were repelled, but four Kuwaiti soldiers were killed. The Bedouin farmers were frightened by the battle at their doorstep, and for two days their sheep and goats wandered without responsible herding.

The contingent of U.S. soldiers was quietly increased at Camp Doha on the outskirts of the city, but there was no clear plan to confront the threat. The nature of the menace was not clear.

Rumors circulated among us that Esau was somehow near the center of criminal activity in the community. The board of directors of Al Ahli Bank moved to dismiss Esau from the board, and there was temporary relief among the Christian community. But the respite was short-lived. Esau had enough well-off supporters for the bank's attempt at his dismissal to be defused. When he passed us on the Gulf Road in his Ferrari F12, he looked pointedly at me and smiled. *What did he plan next? Why didn't he just use physical violence against us? What malevolence was greater than what we had already seen?*

Esau quit his position at the Al Bader Trading Company and opened his own computer-consulting firm. He was a determined and ruthless avenger, moving from victim to victim. The idea that Esau would have such significant computing power at his disposal was anathema to the Kuwaiti Christian community. If indeed it was Esau's intent to ferret out Christians and their proselytizing, then he now had the tools to do so.

Given that Esau had ties to both ISIL and ultra-conservative Islamist groups in Saudi Arabia, he was considered the most visible threat to the Kuwaiti Christian community. He had already informed me explicitly of his intent. Because he had spoken to me directly on the matter, I considered it my responsibility to take up the challenge, but I was at a loss to the method. However, I was not helpless. Esau may have had power, but so did I: power – intelligence, skills, and determination to combat him. *This was my task and mine alone. I would do what was necessary.* Or so, I thought.

I didn't want to go outside my father's authority, so I asked him about the next steps. He was far ahead of me. Once more we sat in the garden of our Ahmadi home, still enjoying my mother's garden and the placid spirit remaining there.

"Papa, you're correct about Esau. He's set himself up as the kingpin here in Kuwait against Christians. It seems like he's doing it all by himself."

"Yes, but that's only part of the problem. He has the backing of Kuwaiti Islamist groups and ISIL. They're active on many fronts and no one knows what they intend to do here in Kuwait. Perhaps it's only minimal or perhaps they intend to move into the area in full force, just like they did in Syria, Iraq, Libya and Yemen. ISIL has confronted Christian groups before, but the Christians melted away. We have no place to retreat."

"If retreat is not an option, what do we do?"

"First, Yusef, you must know in your heart that the Lord is with you. That's the key." *I had no response.* I understood the principle my father stated. My question was: *What can I do?* Of course the Lord was with us. He empowered me, gave me a mission to fulfill. But did I not have to shoulder this responsibility myself anyway? My inner conflict grew, and outwardly…

Our fears were confirmed: Esau did have ties to ISIL-connected groups. What he intended to do with these connections was not yet revealed, but we would at least be aware in advance through Binyamin's computer encroachment into Esau's system. My own fears, however, were not quelled by these small victories. I didn't know what to expect from the Lord. My mother's psalms reminded me of sure refuge. "O Lord my God, in you do I take refuge; save me from all my pursuers and deliver me" (Psalm 7:1). But my refuge was still my own skills, and I expected the worst.

And then there was Esau's Iran connection, which was so far known only to me. Although we had physically removed him from Iran, questions about his contacts there remained. And the bomb? Where was it?

ISIL attacks from the south continued for nearly a year, well into 2022. Only *Al-Jazeera* reported these attacks. All subsequent battles took the same form, and it was clear to the people and the government that the motivation was anti-Christian. The beach houses which they sacked along the southern coast just north of Nuwaiseeb were all owned by Christians. The government was in no position to adjust the political aspects of the discussion. Any attempt to do so would result in the country giving into either the Islamist or the Christian elements. Additionally, the effectiveness of the Christians, led by my half-brother Thawab, in serving in defense of the country was impossible to ignore. Finally, the ISIL forces stopped their attacks and moved on to other Gulf countries where similar events were taking place. By this time the new Pence administration had negotiated a peace agreement between Hamas and the Israelis, and world news was deflected from the Gulf's troubles. Growth of the Gulf Christian community became our primary focus.

I dreamed an unlikely dream, that Jesus would sweep the Gulf. I saw churches filled with Arab converts, heard old Western hymns sung to Arab rhythms. Charles Wesley would have been shocked by the oud with its differing scales. When I awoke I denied the possibility, even knowing what I had seen in Kuwait. In fact, the process was well underway even as I negated the dream. I should have considered our recent successes in my thoughts, but political events in Kuwait swept me up before I grasped their significance. *Why was I so slow in seeing God's plan? What part of me blocked my vision of the Big Picture? Was it my sin, my unbelief, or simply ignorance?*

CHAPTER 16

DISASTER REDUX

Another call from Esau, never a good omen for the next event. "Meet me tonight at seven – at the Mais Alghanim. Reserve a table for four. I'm bringing wives." Click, end of contact. I obeyed, but I didn't subject my family to knowledge of the ordeal.

Seven in the evening at the restaurant, on the second floor, no Esau. His technique of being late to elevate anxiety had played out with me, and I sat drinking tea, nodding periodically to the waiter indicating the nearing appearance of my guests. I knew he'd arrive eventually.

At 8:30 the trio finally appeared. His two wives wore the traditional Bedouin garb of black abaya and niqab. The flowing abaya concealed any evidence of their form, and the niqab covered their faces except for the eyes, which were heavily made up with mascara and eye shadow. This Kuwaiti attire was much the same as the chadors they had worn in Iran. Their eyes were almost black, dazzling. Esau introduced me to Almira and Laleh, who spoke to me for the first time in English, both with a British accent.

Almira began, "Yusef, are you glad to see us again? We see you didn't bring your friends this time." A little sarcasm.

Laleh joined her. "Do you think you can manage us by yourself?" And then a giggle.

Their voice inflections were soft without a hint of anger, and their eye contact, normal. Here we were, a quiet foursome conversing in a big restaurant across Gulf Road from the sea, reading an extensive menu of Lebanese dishes, for all appearances friends who had no serious past and an agreeable future. Then falafel, hummus, and tabbouleh. They all chose lamb kofta for their meat dish.

Due to their verbal expression and relaxed manner in what I thought for them was a novel situation, and their familiarity with foods other than Persian, I wondered who these women really were. *Where were they from?* Surely they were not the religious dupes of the Persian theocracy I had expected. *And why the connection to Esau and his plan, whatever it was? Had they been merely posing as Basij in Tehran?*

"You're wondering about the reason for our little gathering, and admiring my wives, Almira and Lelah, aren't you?" Esau leaned back in chair, smiled vaguely, stroking his beard. At least he didn't laugh at me. "You must know by now that they're British." I had no response. "Well, here is a bit more information for you. This is bigger than Kuwait and bigger than Iran. There are others too, who are sick to death of the religious skullduggery here in your Middle East, every brand of it." He pulled himself forward in the chair, leaning on the arms for support. "We're against all of you – Christians, Muslims, both Sunni and Shia, and of course the Jews, but they're too few to count. You and your ilk are responsible for all the evil in the world. Anything you don't like, you identify as sin." He kept his voice low, which made it somehow all the more threatening. His wives were silent. "By your saying you're opposed to sin, you've created it. There is no sin. There's only self-interest. And my interest, our interest, is getting rid of all you religious flunkies." He covered his mouth so he wouldn't be overheard or lip read. "We have a growing group, based in Britain, which has the same goal."

The hummus and kibbeh arrived, and the Philippine waiter filled our tea cups.

"We're funded by the Russell Civilization, a name we keep to ourselves for security. We use Bertrand Russell as our icon, a model of one who rejected all religion."

"There was much more to Russell than that. It's not fair to his memory."

"Do you think we're concerned about his memory? We take the money if his followers give it, and they don't understand what we're all about anyway." The three, in unison, leaned back from the table after their last remark. The main dishes arrived, and they dived in. I didn't feel like eating.

"I'm sure you can see, my brother, that all this is far from over." Then, no more information during the meal. My three companions finished up with baklava while I had a Turkish coffee. Then, they rose and departed, leaving me with the bill.

Only outside in the carpark did I learn more. Esau was waiting by my car, his two wives were already in the front seat of his Mercedes. "Yacoub, this is the part I avoided in the closeness of the restaurant. Your bomb is here in Kuwait now. You'll hear soon what we need from you. Good night." With that, he drove off.

CHAPTER 17

PAYING THE PIPER

I didn't get it. *How could God do this? Was He doing this to me as punishment for my sin in helping Iran get a bomb? Was I important enough to matter this much? How could Esau get back in the picture so cleanly, and with the bomb again?* Surely there were connections in Iran I did not know. *What was Esau's real goal? Was it financial gain or was he telling the truth with all that anti-religious talk?* Sooner or later, there must be a price to pay. *I had no answers.*

The bill was delivered in two days via a means I hadn't considered. A courier from the Emir arrived at our villa in Ahmadi at 7 p.m. with a message commanding me to come to the palace the next morning. My thoughts went back to myself: likely he wanted to commend me for my brave sojourn in Tehran, a Kuwaiti citizen who had risen in triumph over the oppressor. It was about time. The story of my life: a hero without an heroic act.

I arrived at the Seif Palace at 9 a.m., and was ushered through a series of intermediaries, each at a higher level, until we reached a small sitting room where the ancient Emir Sabah sat, an attendant by his side. The attendant helped Sabah rise on his cane, and I gave the customary kiss on each cheek, whereupon the ancient

Emir collapsed back in his chair and with a sigh dismissed the attendant. No others were present.

He motioned for me to pull my chair near to him as he gave me permission to sit. "Young man, you had yourself quite a time during your Persian so-called incarceration. Depending on how you handle your current misadventure, you may receive a state medal. But that is only one of several possibilities."

"Thank you, your Highness."

He looked at me directly and didn't speak for a moment. *My proper response to what might be a threat?*

"My young friend, I have, via diplomatic courier, received a letter from the head of the Iranian Ministry of Economic Affairs and Finance, Karim Khadim. It seems you were involved in complex interactions during you stay in Iran." He leaned back in his chair, awaiting my reply.

"My time there was difficult, filled with choices I didn't want to make." No more admission than necessary.

"Well, it seems so. Let me read: 'To the honored Emir of the State of Kuwait, Sabah Al-Ahmad Al-Jaber Al-Sabah: In the name of Allah, I regret I must inform you of the dishonest and illegal activities of one your citizens, Yusef Al-Tamimi. Mr. Al-Tamimi, while an honored guest in our country, procured a nuclear weapon for nefarious and illegal use. He operated in this endeavor with one Esau Allison. I do not know the location of this weapon in question, but you should concern yourself that it may be in your lovely and worthy country.'"

I fell back in my seat, lips numb. "It seems, Yusef, that we have reached an impasse that only you can breach."

My mind whirred. Khadim again. Even in Tehran, I had wondered about his seeming lack of knowledge about the missing bomb. *How could he fail to know?* The answer was now clear: *He had known from the beginning.*

"I want an answer from you within two weeks. You may leave." My role defined itself. The Lord had thrust me into something too difficult for me.

I had to contact Khadim. I booked a flight on Kuwait Airways the next day. On arrival at Khomeini airport, I took the taxi directly to Saleh Hosseini Street and proceeded to Khadim's office. No time to delay. His assistant, sitting outside his office, recognized me. *Was I expected?* I was ushered in to see Khadim without delay.

Papers strewn over the office, desk and floor, cigarette hanging from his lips, tie and shirt collar open, all common characteristics for Khadim. He glanced up from his computer. "What took you so long? Let's get to it."

What was the "it"?

"Surely you didn't think Allison could get the bomb all by himself. We're partners, Esau and I, and now you're the third." *This was already far worse than I thought it would be.*

It was then I pulled out the thumb drive, the one I had kept recording his illegal transfers from all the bond disposals. He plugged it in his computer, paled, and gave the drive back to me. "I'm sure you have other copies. Otherwise you'd be headed back to Evin. Hear me out though first. I'm no more a Muslim than you are. I'm just like Esau – antireligious. Yes, you can hurt me with your little thumb drive, but think of what I may do to you."

Khadim then proceeded to give a too-detailed-and-painful-for-me explanation. He and Esau had made their plan around the time I had procured the nuclear weapons. Khadim had shuffled their paperwork around in such a way that he had created a bomb shell game, so that the whereabouts of all the weapons was known only to him. Thus, it was no problem to set aside one of the bombs for their own vile purpose. In essence, no one else actually knew this bomb existed. The only question was how to use the weapon to achieve their aim: the destruction of any and all religious movements in the Middle East. Khadim went to speak to his secretary, as I sat dumbfounded and in shock.

I had been a fool. I had come to Iran as a shallow Christian believing I could make a difference, but really relying on myself more than God. Along with the dreams of Jesus, I thought I was a star, with my insightful interpretations and the like. Now I was in the center of a mess designed to eliminate religion altogether. *What had I done? Reality pierced me to the marrow. I felt ill. I would be the one, not remembered for my wisdom and skill in encouraging others to know Christ, but for the destruction of His people.* Ashamed and emptied, I bowed my head, aghast.

But I was not alone. When my pride finally submitted itself to God, He met me in an instant. In my mind's eye, I saw Jesus sweeping through the Gulf as He had in my recent dream. I blessed my mother for those psalms she had forced me to memorize as Psalm 2:4 echoed in my mind: "He who sits in the heavens laughs." Indeed, the Bible said the Lord scoffed at His enemies. Only God was in charge of this, not me. I never was. Not then and not now. Further, God was not shocked and surprised about this great threat to His own. What was the solution? I did not know. Finally, I saw I had to wait on the Lord.

Khadim told his secretary to cancel his remaining appointments and returned. "Here's the plan: Our story is that the bomb has been planted in Kuwait City by Christians as an example to Muslims in the Middle East. You may go home and inform your ancient Emir of the same. Then, we'll see what happens." Khadim dismissed me with a hand flourish. As I left, he packed his black leather briefcase for an early departure for the day, perhaps a reward to himself for a job accomplished.

I took the next flight to Kuwait. *Who would be blamed if the bomb exploded in Kuwait? I knew the answer to that question all too well.*

CHAPTER 18

GO FETCH THAT BOMB

As I pulled out of the Kuwait airport carpark, my eyes snapped from one large building to another. Where would they put the bomb? As if I could figure it out by guessing. *What came next? Where was the answer?* Esau had no reason to tell me anything, so there was no point in contacting him. No, the answer still had to be with Khadim, but how to get it from him? After I proceeded though the gate of our Ahmadi home, I found my father sitting in the flower garden planted by mother. He held his head high to catch the fragrance.

"How was your trip?" Surely no sarcasm from my father. At first I couldn't muster a response but my explanation, overly clear, spoiled his afternoon. Mine too. "Yusef, you have the upper hand." *Why hadn't I seen this?* "If he betrays your secret, it's embarrassing to you, but your secret about him could result in his confinement and probably execution." Courage rose slowly, so slowly, in my heart.

My father was correct. It was just another example of my lack of courage. *How could I have failed to see this during my recent meeting with Khadim? I had been too overwhelmed with my own shame.* I had to throw down the challenge to Khadim and bring this matter to an end. By the next morning, my pluck was up, but there was no point in returning to Tehran to threaten Khadim. A text was enough. "Do what you will. If you don't assist me, I'll release the info on your bond money diversion."

Two hours passed with no response. Then a possible surrender, "I'll text you the location tomorrow. The detonation is scheduled in two days. It will happen. There's nothing you or I can do. We'll see you're blamed, if you're still alive." *What a mess. I had delayed too long.*

Another night of uncertainty and then the location: Al-Masjid Al-Kabir, the Grand Mosque, the site designed to yield the greatest symbolic message, the worst possibility for the Christians who were to be blamed. How could we stop the explosion? I called on Thawab for help. Could he interrupt the process already set in motion, and then deal with the bomb itself? I didn't want Thawab involved. I was still jealous of him, but he was my best option.

When Thawab and his men arrived at the mosque, Esau was already present and hovering over the weapon, which had been placed in the innermost location under the large central dome. He pressed the button located on the rear third of the gray weapon, but nothing. He pressed again. Nothing. Esau was apprehended by Thawab and his four men and taken into custody. Thawab knew nothing about the bomb's operation, but God had prevailed. The Kuwaiti Secret Service took possession of the bomb and, after loading it into a brown, unmarked van, drove away rapidly. Where was the bomb headed now? Who was really in charge of it.

Why had the bomb not detonated? *A miracle or another trick?* Khadim had come through in order to preserve his life. He had given the wrong codes to Esau. Khadim still had much to reflect upon, many problems remaining, but this immediate disaster had been averted. I had underestimated all parties on both sides, and overestimated myself as usual. Khadim was the champion-betrayer this round. And did he still have some control over the bomb?

In view of Thawab's apparent, successful intervention, the news media came to interview our family. I explained how Esau had been thrown out of Iran and how he had procured the bomb by his own devices, not an entirely complete or even truthful explanation. I was careful to keep Khadim's name out of it. (I might need him in the future.)

For a brief time, Esau was the focus of scandal. The bomb was one thing, of course, and that was enough, but the current Emir had used Esau as an agent to transfer illicit funds out of Kuwait on many occasions. That was clearly the reason he had been observed on occasion at the palace. However, the Emir's staff leaked information to the newspapers, and it was reported, not accurately, that Esau had been the *sole* instigator of illegal fund transfers. The transfers had been in progress for much longer than Esau's tenure, and under the thumb of the Sabahs as well. Binyamin had already uncovered much of this information.

In addition to Esau's being the instigator of the recent bomb crisis, the Emir set up Esau as the financial culprit. In the Emir's plot to regain control of the situation, Esau became the fall guy for all the ills of Kuwait. He was taken by security forces with camera entourage to the airport, placed on a flight to New York, and summarily deported. He had the haggard look of a trapped thief on his way to prison. His poor family with his two wives and six children were left crying behind the airport window of the departure area. Our Al-Tamimi family watched this televised spectacle, happy it was finally over, but sad for his family. It was the end of a great spiritual soccer match, but we were thankful it was done.

The Prime Minister of Kuwait went on TV, where he delivered a most unusual speech. Until this time, the royal family had never bothered to explain anything to the citizens. "My fellow Kuwaitis, I must sadly report we had a thief and killer among us, one Esau Allison. Unbeknownst to us, he has systematically stolen funds from our oil revenues. He has carried out this theft through computer hacking for many years and taken much from us. We have discovered this after his role in an attempt to set off a nuclear weapon in our country was reported. He has been deported and the matter is now brought to a close." The Prime Minister thus made it seem that Esau was the thief and not the Sabahs themselves. That Esau could not have done the fund transfers without the Emir's approval was obvious to all. Minister Nawaf's explanation failed in any logical sense, but the great mosque and the country were freed of the bomb.

For the time being, Esau's Kuwait career was finished. The Emir and Prime Minister did not wish to deal further with Esau for reasons that remained obscure to me. He was ceremoniously flown to the United States, his arrival there huge in the Kuwait TV evening news, cameras on hand at the airport. But the bomb or its presence in Kuwait was never explained. Would I be connected?

Since Esau was still a U.S. citizen, Nawaf said Kuwait didn't want to get involved in his prosecution. A local trial would have been the proper way of handling the situation, but his immediate expulsion avoided any more output of information. Suddenly, and with no direct action on our part, we were rid of at least one vermin, at least for the present.

CHAPTER 19

THE LORD PROCEEDS WITH HIS PLAN

In the midst of the preservation of Kuwait from the nuclear weapon and the failing ISIL probes, my family resumed its rise to prominence. My father said, "We've not been so respected since the days before oil. And now it's because our country is under attack by ISIL and Iran." I nodded at my father's irony.

My father was right. The Al-Tamimi promotion came first through the military success of Thawab. His photograph, with jaunty military hat, multicolored medals, and high boots, graced the front page of the *Kuwait Times*. Thawab was taller than his comrades, and always managed to be in the foreground. I was put off by his achievements, first in the church and now in the military. After all, I had been the favored son. Hibah called me to task about my self-centered attitude. "Yusef, as our mother would have said, 'You're doing it again.'" I dropped my chin. She was right.

Gradually, as ISIL moved out of the immediate picture in Kuwait, Thawab's photo appeared less often. Attention turned to me when I least felt the need for it. My taste for fame had dulled, but after Esau was gone because of my imprisonment in Iran, I became somewhat of a folk hero. The ill will between Iran and the Arab side of the Gulf served to exaggerate my role. These were strange reasons for fame, which I now shrugged off. In contrast to my former modus operandi, I found I no longer needed or wanted the adulation of others. *Had the Lord removed that burden from me?* I was also developing a respect for my brother. I needed to get to know Thawab, and it was not too late.

I had wandered to Iran to pursue my own ideas of success and created problems for myself instead. This had set off the Esau skirmish in the process. The fortune I anticipated there never materialized, but I had heard the dream stories, and they left their mark on me, just as they had on those who had dreamed.

A shift occurred within my heart. I recalled my mother's dying words: "my soul thirsts for you; my flesh faints for you" (Psalm 63:1). Even with her last breath, she had sought God. I looked for answers inside myself, but the answers were elsewhere. I saw that now more clearly than ever. The knowledge that the solutions were external freed me. God could be trusted with my future, and the future of little Kuwait. I couldn't.

I was interviewed on the Kuwaiti television station, Al Araby.

My assertion, "No, I don't want makeup," was ignored, and the makeup man dabbed my face. I was unaccustomed to the odd sensation of a man's touch on my face. The lights of the TV studio burned bright, and I was concerned the makeup would melt.

My experiences in Evin prison provoked the greatest interest. Although there were details I would not share, the impression that emerged elevated my position. The TV interviewer asked foolish questions. "Were you afraid at Evin?"

Of course I was afraid, every hour, every minute. "Yes, there were days I was afraid," I responded. If it happened again, would I fear? "Yes, of course, but I would no longer depend on myself for the remedy." My confidence had shifted to Jesus, by the working of the Spirit. "No, I never wanted to return to Evin; but if I did, with God's help, I would tear up any letter offering me the coward's cup."

"Tell us what it was like at Evin."

"The prison was a place of torture. We never knew what they would do to us next. One brand of torture would end only to be replaced by another." I shared nothing of my life living amid the pleasant bustle of the city in a Tehran apartment.

"What did you do during those long days and months in prison?"

"I prayed for release. I prayed for my family." In actual fact, prayer had comprised a tiny fraction of my time there.

"Tell us about the torture." He wanted gore for his viewers.

"The psychological torture was the worst." This was true, because it was, in a way, self-inflicted, not God-caused or prison-caused. I refused to elaborate on the physical torture. The interviewer looked disappointed, and I imagine his viewers switched channels.

I didn't disclose that I spent most of my time on the streets of Tehran, all the while carrying out deeds that were traitorous to Kuwait and the rest of the world. I was a hero through non-heroic acts, which is the story for most "heroes." *My mother was a real hero: She had depended on Someone beside herself. Now, I knew the difference.*

The peculiar result of my imprisonment and the TV appearance was an exposure of my personal appeal, which was for me an unneeded, unwanted affirmation, completely undeserved. I knew the praise was foolish, and I lapped it up (the old habit); but I began to see God's purpose in these events as they unfolded before me.

Hibah came to me the next day as I sat in the garden by the yellow *arfaj* blossoms. "Several I spoke with yesterday saw you on TV. I forgot how winning you can be. As your sister, I don't really think about it, but it was pointed out to me again by my friends, and TV brings it out. I'm curious. Did you wear makeup? Your skin looked so smooth." Now she was laughing at me. Just like a sister.

"Why are you telling me this? You know I don't need any compliments."

"I'm fully aware of that, but God has a purpose for you, or He wouldn't have designed you this way. You've seen how prominent Thawab has become. Any of this is only good if it serves the Lord's purpose. I think you should enter into politics here in Kuwait. If a known Christian could win a seat in the parliament, then

242

who knows where it might lead." She came near me and placed her hand on mine as we sat together on the iron garden bench. She loved me for all my faults, and finally I saw those crevices, too.

"I'm not going in that direction," I answered quickly, perhaps too quickly.

"Whose desire are you following? What's your direction? We know what happened in Iran. Even as a prisoner, you achieved much, though we don't know the results yet. You must think about the whole picture and God's plan. If you don't join His work, then He'll get someone else." She lifted her hand from mine.

For a week I said nothing more about Hibah's words, but thought of little else. I thought back to my dream about Jesus sweeping the Gulf and how I had rejected it as an impossibility. I remembered how God had brought it to my mind again in Khadim's office. Once more I envisioned the services crowded with Jesus worshippers, the overflowing parking lots, the stacks of Bibles being plucked up.

I was of two minds: I loved the attention and feared the cost. But my spirit began to change. For God it must have been agonizingly slow. I was a slow student of faith. Hibah was gentle, but prompting. "Yusef, you know you have a role." *Was my confidence in the Lord increasing?* Perhaps.

Then Mohammed Al-Bader from the National Democratic Alliance phoned me on my cell. How did he get my number? Hibah had apparently contacted him through her connections at the university. "Yusef, we want to support you for parliament." He proposed my candidacy in the Ahmadi district with the support of his party, but there were complicating factors. The party's constituency was Muslim, which was no surprise, but there were other differences as well, not the least of which was their hard line policy against Iran. Despite my experiences in Iran's prisons, I still held a positive view of the country and its people. The party's favorable view of women and popularity among younger Kuwaitis appealed to me, and frankly I had no other good options. The idea of running for office was both a curse and delight for me.

The campaign was rougher than anticipated. The main opposition candidate, Ri'ad Al-Hasawi, dug into my family's history. My chief regret was his muckraking attacks on my father as he reminded everyone of my father's flight from Kuwait during the Iraqi invasion more than thirty years earlier. He was quoted, "Yusef was spawned by a coward. How can he be any different than his deserter father?" Such was the language of the campaign.

My father didn't care. "Let them say what they say." He sat in his great chair reading Mahfouz's Cairo trilogy, the *Sugar Street* volume. He didn't want to be disturbed. He was long past any remaining guilt over the matter.

The next attack was on Hibah for her active, vocal, and successful legal defense of two Christians who had fallen into the clutches of the Kuwaiti court system. Likewise, Hibah was unperturbed, and I suspect what was most upsetting for the opposition was her triumph in that defense. But the greatest threat to my candidacy and me came from an outside source. The e-mail arrived on October 22, 2021, two weeks before the election:

"Dear Yusef,

I know it has been a long time since we spoke, and now I am no longer a child. I owe you much for explaining my dream and procuring a Bible for me. You told me to keep my belief in Jesus secret, and for a long time I was able to do so. But the secret is out, and my little family and I are in danger. (I am married now to a beautiful believing wife and we have one small child.) There are many believers in Iran, and they are allowed their religious freedom as long as their families don't interfere. As you know, my parents are strong Muslims, and my conversion is considered apostasy. My father has agreed to have me killed, and I fear this sentence will be carried out soon. Can you help me somehow? I must get out of Iran. I have tried and cannot get a visa for the United States or Europe, and even if I could, I would be blocked at the airport here in Isfahan or certainly in Tehran. I don't know what to do or where else to turn.

Afsin"

His request could not have come at a more difficult time, yet I felt responsible. How could I get him and his family to Kuwait? As an Iranian, he would not be eligible for Kuwaiti citizenship. Only a job would provide him legal residence here. God had given Afsin's conversion, in part, as a gift to me; and now I freely accepted such gifts. And, thank the Lord, fear had left me.

My father's old business, the Kuwait Tool and Electric Company, still existed on paper though my father had not done any real work there in years. Nevertheless, the inactive, but still existing,

245

family business could provide him the contract qualifying him for residence.

The biggest problem was actually getting him to Kuwait. He was unable to fly from any airport in Iran. Through my old contacts in the Iranian nuclear workforce, I arranged a small boat departing out of the Bushehr port on the night of October 30. Their arrival on the craft *Scheherazade* in the Kuwait harbor near the center of town went unnoticed two nights later. They pulled in next to the yachts and got off onto the wharf like any Kuwaiti family returning from a day at sea. I had instructed Afsin in the proper dress for such an appearance, and he wore the traditional gray dishdasha and red-and white-checkered keffiyeh as a head-dress. I met them by the boats where the small fish swam in the clear water illuminated by the bright lights of the dock.

Even though years had passed, the bearded, grown man I greeted stunned me. We embraced briefly, both of us concerned about creating a scene. Hibah and I took them to a small hotel near the Hilton.

Because of their covert arrival, their passports did not have an entry stamp. Hibah was able to clear this problem through friends in the immigration office. The required physical examination for the residency permit required three trips to the Shuwaikh Port office. There the little family received the same torment that most non-Western ex-patriot families had to endure, but finally they had residency permits, and with those, they could purchase a car. Kuwaiti Christians pulled together the necessary funds to get them started. There were finally enough Christians in Kuwait that someone could be called upon to assist others in such surprising circumstances. Afsin was embarrassed and stunned by the help and gifts. "I never hoped for all this."

Hibah had done her work with efficiency. "We don't want anything to interfere with your candidacy. We'll keep all this quiet," she commented.

We thought we could rest on this, but somehow the newspaper got hold of the story, and I was accused of smuggling Christians into the country. When publicly confronted with this charge, I agreed it was true. "Yes, I have assisted political refugees fleeing Iran." My popularity was only enhanced! *How could even this event have worked for my success?* The Lord had truly visited me.

There were thirty-two candidates for parliament in the Ahmadi area. The top ten candidates that gathered the highest votes would gain seats in the parliament. Because I was the only candidate who admitted to being a Christian, the thirty-one other candidates were united against me. The most popular, Al-Hasawi, was selected by the group to debate with me on Kuwait TV. Although not intended by me or stated by others, the main area of debate was religious. The selected debate coordinator was a known Islamist. He had a long, black, furry beard and a severe expression. There would be few smiles from him toward me. Early in the debate it became clear that the ground rules were to be abandoned in favor of a hostile environment. The seat I was given in the TV studio was wobbly and the lights were purposely directed in my eyes. Hasawi got makeup; I got none.

In order to differentiate myself clearly, and at the suggestion of Hibah, I wore a business suit. Al-Hasawi wore the traditional dishdasha.

The coordinator began by questioning me. "Mr. Tamimi, let's set the record straight: Are you a Christian?"

"Yes, I am a Christian." *Finally, I really was too! I could say this with clarity and pride.* "But we are here today, I believe, to discuss the political future of Kuwait. The religious future is under the direction of Allah. Is that not correct?"

The coordinator then turned smiling to Al-Hasawi, "Mr. Hasawi, do you believe religion affects the politics of Kuwait, and, if so, how?"

"Our traditions are Islamic and as such, we rely on the precedents set by our forerunners when any outcome of law is decided. The basis for our legal system is Sharia law."

Al-Hasawi clearly did not understand the Kuwait legal system. I responded as gently as possible. "I am afraid Mr. Hasawi is incorrect. Our Kuwaiti system of law is actually a combination of civil law, or codified law, and Islamic law. As such, precedents play little role in court decisions. The great wisdom of our Kuwaiti fathers has been the moderation of our system of government, not its strictness. We must stand for both justice and mercy."

Seeing the weakness of Al-Hasawi in understanding our country's legal system, the coordinator redirected the questions to more specific areas relating to government services. "Mr. Hasawi, what area do you think requires the most improvement among the basic needs of our people?"

"The basic needs of our people lie in the area of religion and ethics. Our lives must be grounded in Islamic principles. Anything that erodes Islam lessens the will and determination of our people." Once again he attempted to turn the debate to religion. The debate coordinator shook his head at Al-Hasawi when he was off-camera.

"Mr. Tamimi."

"As Mr. Hasawi must know, the behavioral dictates of Islam and Christianity are virtually identical. If these are obeyed; then the outcome, from the standpoint of being a good citizen, should be identical. But we are not in a religious debate." At that point I looked at Hasawi who was straightening his keffiyeh off-camera. I don't think he even heard me.

I went on about the requirements of the people. "To answer your question about the basic needs of our people, I want to focus on more practical matters, which include electricity, water, and food expenses. Allah blesses us here in Kuwait. We have abundant financial and geological resources, and there is no excuse for any Kuwaiti to ever lack any of these basic needs. As members of parliament, we must protect the citizens against diversion of funds from these needs."

The coordinator continued, "Mr. Hasawi, what is your biggest concern about the outcome of the coming election?"

"I'm worried about the influence of women as voters. Will they change the dynamic of the outcome? Can they be trusted with our future?" The coordinator jumped in and cut off Hasawi before he damaged himself any further with half the electorate.

I took advantage of the blunder. "We must respect the views and participation of all our citizens." And so it went. The debate was terminated early so that Hasawi would not be completely discredited. He had demonstrated a minimum understanding of the debate process and even the newly enfranchised electorate.

Both Hasawi and I were elected to the parliament. This achievement was not surprising. I stood third in the voting, thanks primarily to the women's vote. Hasawi was second. As the first Christian ever elected to office in Kuwait, I understood that my personal qualities had nothing to do with the victory. The Psalms, the Psalms of my mother, reminded me of the certainty of what God ordained. God gave me more than I had requested, more than I prayed for.

The execution of His plan would not be without strife for me, but I had at last settled to His will.

CHAPTER 20

THERE WOULD BE NO REST

The *Kuwait Times* and the *Kuwait Daily News* both made my status as a Christian the main topic of the election. The *Kuwait Times* editorial read: "The election to parliament of Yusef Al-Tamimi, a known Christian, is a sign of change in Kuwait, a change for the worse. His election represents an erosion of Islamic values. The question for all Muslims is whether this trend can be reversed before it takes hold. We do not wish Mr. Al-Tamimi any ill-will, but we must wonder about his safety and the safety of his family in this situation." *Was this last sentence a threat?*

The *Daily News* was more forthright. "The election of Mr. Al-Tamimi has brought impending disaster upon our Islamic state. We are the laughingstock of the Gulf. Our sacred duty requires that we correct the error." If this had been said about any other member of parliament, the paper would have been sanctioned.

That evening after midnight there was an explosion outside the wall of our Ahmadi home. The sudden, ground-shaking blast awakened us, and we all hurried into the living room. We inspected each other, thankful there were no injuries. While none of us were harmed, the explosion brought the threat into focus. The explosion was punctuation to the newspaper articles. We agreed we should stay together in the living room and called the police. My father slumped in his chair, head down, fingers folded together and prayed quietly.

The police pulled up two hours later, no lights or sirens. All that time we had been waiting, wondering, fidgeting, wanting to know if we were under an attack. The investigating officer said, "We will not find those who did this. Perhaps you should leave." The police departed without investigating, and I went outside the wall myself. The explosives had been a bundle of fireworks contained in a box nearly a meter in all dimensions – large enough to cause a terrific blast, but not enough power to destroy the wooden box, which had been placed so it wouldn't cause any real damage. It was a warning, meant to frighten us, which it did. I didn't get back asleep until 7 in the morning.

At 8 o'clock, there was a phone call from CNN for me. They wanted an interview. No, the caller said, he had not heard about the explosion. The interview request was about my election to the Kuwaiti Parliament and the fact that I was a Christian. I just couldn't tolerate another invasion of any sort, and I cut the conversation short with a quick, "I'll get back to you."

Thirty minutes later there was a knock at the door. A messenger from *Al Jazeera* greeted me. "Mr. Al-Tamimi, we want to interview you about your election." Before I could dismiss the young man, Hibah overheard.

"Yusef, you must take the interview." She stepped in front of me and told the messenger I could do the interview that afternoon. I glared at her, but it was too late; the messenger was gone with her acceptance. The Lord used Hibah to give me wise direction.

"Look, Hibah, I've already put off CNN. I just don't want any more news. I don't want any more explosions. I want to be left at peace for a while." But peace, at least not by my standard, was not the Lord's plan.

"You must take the interviews. Call CNN back right now. Something important has happened here, and we can't let the chance go. I know you're worn out. We all got only an hour of sleep last night, but the time is here and you must take advantage of it." She was not going to quit, and I was too drained to argue. The Lord gave me the power to comply.

The first interview was with CNN, and occurred via televised transmission from our home with the questions presented from the CNN headquarters. The questions were sensationalized rather than insightful, and the questioner was more interested in presenting his own views than in collecting information from me. "Mr. Al-Tamimi, I can imagine how fulfilled you must be in your unique election to the Kuwaiti Parliament. Please tell us about your family's experiences." *Did he want to hear about the bombing?*

"Well, we are of course very happy with the results—" My response was interrupted before I could bring up the bombing. The fake bomb was heavy on my mind, and the interviewer didn't know about it. His focus was not the same as mine.

"I'm sure this result means a new day for Kuwait. Your country has begun a trend that sets it apart from the rest of the Gulf. You must be excited and proud your country has shown its new mindset of political freedom." I considered myself an anomaly and not a trend. Only the Lord knew the trend.

"Actually, I don't think we can yet be certain of such a change, but—" By now I was used to being interrupted. I was going to follow my "but" with a "thanks to the Lord," but CNN was not interested.

"We at CNN are all impressed by your country's courage." *What about mine, my new courage?*

Interruption after intrusion. The reporter got his views across effectively, but never heard mine. Hibah observed, "At least he had great hair." I smiled.

The *Al-Jazeera* interview was different. Suddenly, the vision of the beautiful young woman, Tahara Al-Thani, appeared in front of me, this time for real. She arrived at our home in the late afternoon with a cameraman and set up the interview in our living room. She was even more stunning in person, and I was entranced. It was as if she had stepped out of her newsroom, just to see me. She had. She didn't wear the head covering of the conservative Muslim woman, and her black hair was shining and free of hair spray. Her hair moved when she walked. She was not immodest in any way, but neither did she show the usual inhibitions of the typical Arab woman. She extended her hand to me, gripped my hand firmly, and gave it three shakes. She did this on camera.

"Mr. Al-Tamimi, congratulations on your recent election to the

Kuwaiti Parliament. I've read the text of your debate with one of your opponents, and I'm aware of your general political views, but I want to concentrate on your position as a Christian. I'm certain that will be of the greatest interest to our viewers and readers. First, how did you become a Christian?" There was no longer any reason to hide my faith.

"I was raised in a Christian home. My mother was the first Christian in our family. She became one by reading the Bible. She taught me from my childhood."

"How has being a Christian made your life different?"

This question might have been too difficult for me only a few short months before. I took a deep breath and tried to gather myself. "The Lord is in control of my life. The election has nothing to do with me. I function at His bidding, even though I don't know what's coming next.

The young woman continued on. "How will your religious beliefs influence your political life?"

"In the main, I don't think they will, but in matters of freedom of religion, I intend to defend the basic principle that we are free to choose what we believe."

"What about changing from one religion to another?"

"We should be free to do so."

"I'm sure you know that view is not shared by all."

"A recent court case in Kuwait has addressed this matter. The judge determined that such freedom exists." This was Hibah's case, and what I said was not precisely correct. All that the judge determined was that blasphemy had not occurred.

"Yes, but the real question, as yet unanswered, is apostasy. Where do you stand when the issue is apostasy, not blasphemy?"

She was already aware of the court case and the subtleties of the decision, and she got right to the heart of the matter. Now, I had to say what I thought about a basic freedom. I was of two minds: on the one hand relieved to say what I thought, and on the other frightened of the consequences. But now I sought the Lord's protection, not my own. "There should not be such a charge of apostasy available to the court. One's belief is an individual matter and not a crime." This was a dangerous statement, and in conflict with cultural norms. Both Al-Thani and I knew it. She continued her questions toward less inflammatory areas and closed the interview. We told her about the explosion outside our home, but she left it out of the interview.

Afterward we spoke off record, and she looked me in the eyes. "Mr. Al-Tamimi, I'm truly sorry my question led you to such an answer. To say that apostasy is not a crime puts you in great danger, but you're very brave for saying so. I want you to know I agree with you."

"Well, what's said is said."

"If you want, we'll cut it from the tape."

Before I could respond, Hibah joined in, "No, don't cut it." Her courage vaulted over mine, and for a change I was thankful. I was glad she answered quickly for me, but I couldn't speak. After all, the risk was mine, and I was the one in the line of fire. And so the statement would be heard throughout the Gulf and indeed all the Muslim world.

As she departed, I remarked, "I'm struck by your family name."

"Yes, I'm a distant member of the Qatari royal family. There are many of us. Mr. Al-Tamimi, if you have occasion to come to Qatar, please contact me though *Al-Jazeera*."

Did she say that? I must have misunderstood. An Arab woman would not say that. Perhaps she meant I could tour the *Al-Jazeera* headquarters. *Had we conducted a romance through the TV? Was this all my fantasy?*

Hibah wouldn't let me forget the interviewer's last comment. "Yusef, you must visit her in Doha. I saw how you each looked at the other. And she's a Christian. I'm certain of it. This has all been God's provision. He brought a mate to you. And you put the issue of apostasy out there for all to see and hear. I give thanks to Him."

But Hibah, what about me? What will this cost me? But I did give thanks for this, nevertheless.

My sister must have been able to read my mind. I was stunned by that woman and could see myself marrying her. Yes, I too felt there was a good chance she was a Christian… there was just something about her.

But as for me putting the apostasy issue out there, well, I'd have been happier shutting up about it. But I accepted God's plan now, and not my own. I was caught in the media spotlight. If someone gunned me down, Hibah would be on TV calling me a Christian martyr. In the past I would have resented her interference, but no longer. I was ready, finally, for God's plan.

My *Al-Jazeera* interview hit the Internet the following morning, and the fallout from it followed. While many Islamic writings call for the death penalty for apostasy, as they define it, the views of Quran and Hadith authorities are not clear on this point. And should someone convert from Judaism or some other religion to Islam, then that conversion also met the general definition of apostasy. These and other ideas were discussed.

I came under fire for my Christian testimony; but in addition to the anger against me, the staunch defenders of Islam argued among themselves. The flare-up of the apostasy controversy served to display the unrest intrinsic in the Islam of the day. Should a Muslim kill an unbeliever, a *kefer?* Part of the Quran said yes. Another part of the text called Christians the "People of the Book." I did not know what the future held, but now I knew at last that the Lord was on my side.

My first day in parliament was marked by religious controversy focused on the apostasy question with me in the starring role. Mohammed Al-Fadul rose to speak. "We have among us today one who is an enemy of Islam, and an enemy of our system of law, the great Sharia, one who denies the illegality of apostasy, one who is an enemy of our way of life, a way that has served us well in the Gulf for decades." *Kuwait was not actually under the entirety of*

Sharia law: there were no heads off in the public square, no chop-ping of hands. "This man comes to us as one who says he defends the rights of our people, but in fact he is a traitor to Islam and a traitor to Kuwait. I call on this assembly and indeed on the people of Kuwait to rid us of this dog in our midst, the son of a traitor." Once again my father was brought into the discussion. *Why did my father get hit when they should have been aiming only at me?*

Others in the parliament rose with similar messages. While there was not an explicit call for violence against me, the speeches contained barely veiled threats. My greatest regret was the comment against my father.

Finally, when they had exhausted their ire, all delivered for political effect, I was compelled to present a defense. It was late afternoon, and I was tired from the harangue. My arms swung freely as I approached the podium. "Citizens of Kuwait, I have the greatest respect for my colleagues here in the assembly. I love Kuwait. Kuwait has a long history of respect for the views of all its citizens. Our custom of discussion and reconciliation that is seen in our dīwāniyas is the envy of all other Arab countries. Nowhere is there such unfettered discussion in a forgiving atmosphere. Let us continue to observe the freedom our constitution promises. Let us preserve the peace of Kuwait." The Lord gave me mettle. A photograph of me speaking in Parliament was published widely the next day. CNN interviewed other members of the assembly, and I was accused of sabotaging the country. My mother's psalms defended me when I couldn't defend myself. "Contend, O Lord, with those who contend with me" (Psalm 35:1).

Rather than dealing with questions related to the business of running the country, a bill was introduced dealing with both blasphemy and apostasy. Blasphemy was specifically defined as defaming Islam. Apostasy was defined as leaving Islam. The penalty for both was death. An amendment that it was illegal for a Kuwaiti to be a Christian was narrowly defeated, and without the amendment the bill passed by a wide majority. A bill of the same ilk had been passed by parliament years earlier, and the Emir had quashed it. All involved expected the same outcome, and as expected, the Emir acted to dispose of the measure.

Those in parliament who had spoken out or voted against Christianity had achieved their political aim nevertheless. I had tried to make things better, but believers would suffer. I could only pray He would give them the same courage he had given me.

Two days after the threats in parliament, the physical assault came. Driving back to Ahmadi on King Fahad Bin Abdulaziz Road, two black Lexus sedans passed me. Then, the two vehicles slowed down and blocked both lanes in front of me. A third vehicle pulled up behind and tried to block my exit from the back. My Jeep Patriot was equipped with four-wheel drive, so I turned to the right and into the desert sand. My wheels spun for traction for a moment as two men exited the vehicle in front to my left. Sand flew up into their eyes. They carried pistols with extended clips. Suddenly I heard several rapidly fired rounds of gunfire as they penetrated the side of my car. One round came through the window, striking me in the left shoulder.

It all happened so fast, that at first there was no pain.

Thank God I hadn't been too paralyzed by fear to remain on the road. As I drove through the desert, blood oozed through the dishdasha I had on that day, and onto the seat. I was glad I had leather upholstery rather than cloth. The blood would come off the leather without soaking in. *What a peculiar thought. Could I stay awake until I got to Ahmadi? Were they trying to follow me through the sand?*

I phoned Hibah on the car phone and drove as quickly as possible over the desert sand. On arrival at our home, she drove me to the Ahmadi hospital where several reporters and a TV crew awaited my arrival. Hibah had been efficient in making both the medical and the news arrangements. By that time the wound had become painful, and blood loss and shock were beginning to dull my thoughts. Hibah jumped full force on the whole experience and made the most out of telling the news media about my plight. "My brother was attacked by assassins in the name of Islam. The true nature of this religion is revealed. We expected this, and my brave brother has suffered for the religious rights of all Kuwaitis." I was still alert enough to be concerned about her safety, but she wouldn't soften her tone or comments. I was proud of her, but still afraid for both of us. Hibah fluttered around me like a surrogate mother. She was aflame.

The wound didn't turn out to be serious. It was what the doctor called a through-and-through wound. I was released from the hospital that evening with pain meds and antibiotics. As my mind cleared, I recalled the first three numbers of one of the attacker's license plates, 672. I called the police thinking that a black Lexus with the plate number beginning 672 would not be difficult to locate in the computer system. We never heard any report from the police. The Emir assigned police to accompany me to and from the parliament, but this practice was discontinued after two weeks.

My next encounter with Al-Fadul in parliament pulled me closer to the edge of just getting out of the whole thing. At first, he would not make eye contact. *Why was he even approaching me? What was he trying to tell me? That he had no ill intent?* The mongrel knew what he was doing. Finally, he came near. I muttered, *"Ya kalb"* (you dog). He acted as if he didn't hear me. God kept me from striking him.

"Yusef, I'm truly sorry for your recent experience. I never intended personal harm to you. My comments were for political purposes. I'm sure you know that." *Actually, I did not know this. I felt like knocking him down. He was my enemy. I was sure of it.* But the Lord mediated in my still raucous mind.

"Certainly, Mohammed, I know we're all colleagues in this house of government. I bear you no rancor. Perhaps you can come to our home in Ahmadi for a meal tomorrow evening." He never came. He told others he was afraid to be in the same place with me because of the threats against me. I did not repeat the invitation.

My shoulder healed quickly, but the scar remained. I'm sure God protected me many more times than I know. I varied the route when I drove to parliament. I tied a mirror on a cane I found in my father's closet, and every time I went anywhere, I used this contraption to check for a bomb under my car. I did this only when no one was looking.

Hibah, in contrast, came to breakfast each morning with exhilaration over the day. She thrived on the country's focus on the religious conflict. She went with relish to the paper and TV news each morning. She sprang from one duty to another with oomph, and I was both miffed and thankful for my sister's attitude at the same time. I was the one with the bullet hole.

But Kuwaitis love peace and the pleasure of enjoying their material possessions. Their desire for personal amity and control was their dominant motivation. When I least expected it, everything calmed. I still felt the threat of violence over me, but events did not recur, at least for a time. At a state function the Emir gave me special accord with an eye-to-eye welcome and a nod. I knew the Lord was in all this, a thought I had never experienced at Kashan or Evin.

In January 2022 the Emir appointed me to a committee to seek out a cooperative educational agreement for our graduate students with Qatar. The stated purpose of the visit, the educational agreement, was a subterfuge. The real purpose was a discussion of the Sunni-Shia conflict. Their clash had steadily become more bellicose throughout the Gulf and indeed the whole Muslim world. Would my visit to Doha bring unanticipated changes for me?

Much was unsettled. The bomb we had discovered and disabled

had disappeared. No one in the government would speak of it. How was this possible right before our eyes in Kuwait? Khadim, I suspected, was still at the heart of all this, along with Esau. I even doubted Thawab.

With all the questions – the whereabouts of the bomb, the bomb of my own doing; the presence and eventual deportation of Esau from Kuwait; and this crazy Sunni-Shia conflict, a matter for which I was wholly unprepared – I was still out of Evin Prison and free in Kuwait, and by some miracle elected to the Kuwait Parliament. Sure, the snags between Hibah and me still persisted, but there would be healing. And Binyamin was now a joy to me. How could I be anything but thankful to Him who had brought me this far?

For the time, peace reigned.

And there was my upcoming visit to Doha. Despite the undesirable political aspects of the assignment, Tahara was there.

IF YOU'RE A FAN OF THIS BOOK, WILL YOU HELP ME SPREAD THE WORD?

There are several ways you can help me get the word out about the message of this book...

- Post a 5-Star review on Amazon.

- Write about the book on your Facebook, Twitter, Instagram – any social media you regularly use!

- If you blog, consider referencing the book, or publishing an excerpt from the book with a link back to my website. You have my permission to do this as long as you provide proper credit and backlinks.

- Recommend the book to friends – word-of-mouth is still the most effective form of advertising.

- Purchase additional copies to give away as gifts. You can do that by going to my website at: www.allfaithsoil.com

ENJOY THESE OTHER BOOKS BY JIM CARROLL

Faith in Crisis – How God Shows Up When You Need Him Most, Kuwaiti Seeker, Diwaniya Stories

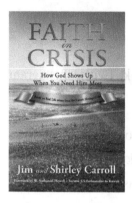 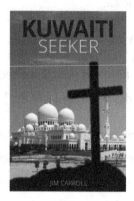 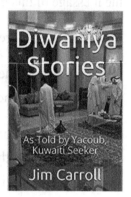

amazon BARNES&NOBLE

You can order these books from AMAZON & B&N or where ever you purchase your favorite books. You can also order these books from my website at: www.allfaithsoil.com

NEED A SPEAKER FOR YOUR NEXT PROGRAM?

Invite me to speak to your group or ministry. I have many years of public speaking experience. If you would like to have me speak to your group or at an upcoming event, please contact me at: www.allfaithsoil.com

AND HERE'S A PREVIEW OF THE THIRD BOOK OF THE EXCITING TRILOGY:

Kuwait and the rest of the Persian Gulf will be turned upside down. And much of the excitement will happen in war-torn Yemen. Two samples follow from the author's personal photos, first the pre-war, old city of Sana'a, Yemen and second, a mountain-top Yemeni city ready for war.

Stay tuned!

The beautiful old walled city of Sana'a before the war

An old hilltop town, ready for attack!